Secret of the Cannon

Careless O'Connor was a remarkable man who, as a frontier agent for the United States Federal Bureau, was only engaged on very important missions. Now his task was to trace the Santa Anna cannon, which had fallen into the hands of the Comanches. Major Abigay had assured him that the cannon had been busted so there was no danger of the Indians causing loss of life as had been the case when they had captured guns previously.

But nothing was quite as it seemed and if the gun was useless why had five other men been trying to trace the weapon with its history dating back to the Napoleonic wars? As always trouble was never far behind Careless and this time he had to face both renegade whites and Comanches on the warpath.

Could even such a doughty fighter as Careless survive against all the odds? Only time would tell!

By the same author

Stampede County

Secret of the Cannon

A Black Horse Western

ROBERT HALE · LONDON

© 1954, 2003 Gordon Landsborough
First hardcover edition 2003
Originally published as
O'Connor Rides In by Mike M'Cracken

ISBN 0 7090 7313 5

Robert Hale Limited
Clerkenwell House
Clerkenwell Green
London EC1R 0HT

Typeset by
Derek Doyle & Associates, Liverpool.
Printed and bound in Great Britain by
Antony Rowe Limited, Wiltshire

ONE

THE LIE!

Everyone was running. It was a rout, suddenly. Blind panic gripped that stockaded frontier town.

A daubed and painted body crashed from the highest firing platform above the gate. It hit the dust and little spirals ascended. It was the first Comanche Indian to fall within the palisade.

But all at once there were hundreds of feathered head-dresses bobbing along the top of those pointed palisade stakes. They were over, swinging within the fortified area by the hundred.

For one moment they were etched against the brilliant blue of the Arizona sky. Then they were running along the firing platforms within the walls.

The defenders, civilians except for those few U.S. gunners, went back to the shelter of the small log buildings that grouped all along the edge of the river. They were firing furiously, incessantly, scarcely able to miss at that close range. And yet they were being driven back, always backwards.

From every point along the palisaded defence agile, war-whooping Indians were pouring into the settlement. Once inside, they began to run towards the big, barred gates – they sought to open them and let in the distant Indian cavalry, waiting with quivering eagerness to join in the assault.

A giant frontiersman, black-bearded and with the sweat rolling in sheets from his brown face, roared, 'Don't le 'em open that gate!' He knew it was the end if the cavalry were allowed to flood in unchecked.

He was thinking, 'This is the end anyway!' He couldn't see any hope for them.

He braced as the big gun boomed again. They had one cannon – a gun captured during the Mexican wars – to defend the settlement. One gun and a newly-arrived gun team, sent out by the United States artillery.

It had been mounted on top of a flat-roofed hut, where it had clearance over the spiked palisade. Black-beard could see the perspiring gunners ramming powder down the muzzle. Only a few were left now – the others had died from the merciless hail of arrows.

Again it roared out, and a ten-pound shot

whizzed towards the distant, waiting cavalry. But big guns weren't much good now. The fighting had become hand-to-hand, and small arms were needed. Only, they hadn't enough.

The end was near. The wounded had been got away across the river – before them, the women and children had been forded across. Smoke began to drift over the tiny town. The Comanches had fired some huts.

Everywhere was white powder snow, drifting bitingly into the faces of the retreating defenders. There was dust, too, every time that big cannon overhead boomed and sent a round shot to harry the distant, waiting horsemen.

Then the Indians reached the main gate and somehow got the mighty bars out of their sockets. They were shot down, but too late.

The gates swung open of their own accord, and at once a charging horde of Indians raced through the narrow opening. They came in with lances held aloft, with war-bonnets streaming behind them, and they came in screaming the high-pitched war cry of the Comanche people.

The big, bearded frontiersman knew it was all over now. He bellowed to his companions to pull out. He didn't attempt to go back with them himself.

He shouted to the grim-faced soldiers up beside their cannon, 'Bust up that gun! Then beat it!'

He didn't want a cannon to fall into the hands of Indians. The last time that had happened, the cannon had been used against American settlers, unprepared, in another frontier outpost.

Then that black-bearded settler prepared to die in order to give his people time to pull out of those buildings and get across that water to their womenfolk and wounded.

He fought like a demon. He raged throughout that little town. And for a long time, he seemed to bear a charmed life.

He fought until his guns were empty. Then he held back the Indians with mighty sweeps of his reversed rifle as they tried to reach the water down a narrow alley. In the end some Indians leaped on him from the roof of a burning building, and then it was all over.

Three minutes before that, a lieutenant had looked at his gun team and then looked at that streaming horde of Indians racing through the newly-opened gate. The lieutenant started to run for the ladder at the back of the hut.

The gun-sergeant remained where he was, the ramrod in his hand. Only he and one other had survived the arrows of the Indians up there on that flat wooden roof.

He shouted, 'The gun!'

The lieutenant turned and began to descend that ladder. His eyes seemed to bite back at the sergeant. He shouted, 'There's no time. Come on man, if you want to save your life!'

The sergeant did. He and the gunner didn't wait to use the ladder. They hung by their hands and then dropped to the ground, and then went racing after their officer towards the water.

When the Indians captured that town they found themselves possessors of a cannon that had never been made in the United States. It was a gun that had been forged in France, captured in a war against Spain, and then brought out to Mexico. Now it had been taken by Indians who didn't know how to use it – yet!

Many white men died in order that others should get through to the eastern bank in safety. When they came out of the water and grouped there, sorry refugees that they were, they saw the town was burning. They saw the victorious Indians riding in and among the buildings, bent on destruction now that everything worth looting had been taken and apportioned among them. They saw the feathered head-dresses, and heard the savage scream of the Comanche war cry.

A settler licked his lips and looked back at the town. He was thinking of the gun that had been brought so laboriously up through New Mexico after it was captured by United States filibusters in the Santa Anna war.

It had seemed security to them, but it hadn't been of great value.

He sighed and said, 'Waal, I guess it won't be

any good to them blamed Injuns.' He wiped the sweat from his smoke-grimed face and looked at the artillery lieutenant. 'I guess you fixed it afore you left, lootenant.'

The lieutenant's eyes flickered and met those of his sergeant. Then he answered, 'I fixed it.'

He was saddled with a lie from that moment. When he reached the nearest army post he entered in his report, 'The gun was rendered useless to the enemy before we left.'

The army made him Major Abigay for that.

A horseman entered the thriving frontier town of Running Squaw late one afternoon. He was big and untidy, and the horse he rode was large and ungainly. They matched, somehow, horse and rider.

The rider dismounted outside the Wells Fargo office. A sign had been tacked up – 'U.S. Army H.Q.' Wells Fargo wouldn't be running any coaches westwards for some time, anyway.

That big, shambling figure shoved back an old hat that was a disgrace on any man. He looked at the sign. He had a big, flat, battered face that had clearly stopped a lot of punches in its time, and yet there was a kind of lazy good humour about it that somehow inspired confidence. His shirt was faded and torn, and his jeans slopped out of riding-boots that had never been cleaned and stood in much need of repair.

Truly he was not a man who cared about appearances.

He looked through the open doorway of the Wells Fargo office and saw an army officer writing at a plank table within. A few hatless, perspiring soldiers were coming in and out of the room with messages. The H.Q. seemed to be pretty busy.

The big *hombre* took out a pipe and then cut off some pieces of tobacco and rolled them and packed them into that old, stained bowl. He lit it, and a passing, tame Indian got the whiff and hurried on, looking sick.

The smoke drifted into the room and bit into the nostrils of that colonel sitting at the table. He pulled a face and began to exclaim, 'Who in heck's set fire to some old cabbage stumps!'

His eyes lifted and he saw that huge, untidy man in the doorway. At once his eyes lighted into a smile. He half-rose, his hand extended in greeting.

'Careless O'Connor, by heck!' he exclaimed.

The big, untidy-looking frontiersman, almost blocking that doorway, removed the villainous old pipe from his mouth and then drawled, 'Less o' the Careless, colonel!'

But there was such good humour in his voice that it ceased to be a rebuke. Having said that, the big *hombre* turned to look at the scene of activity along the main street. Or it might have been the natural caution of a man who looks around always for sight of possible enemies.

The colonel came over to shake his hand, like a man who has met an old friend. He was rather old to be in military service, a fine, straight-looking man with a heavy grey moustache. His grey eyes were narrow and had lines at the corners, like a man who has spent his life in the saddle and faced the Western sun most of that time.

Together they looked along the main street. Everywhere men seemed to be doubling about their business. Horsemen were racing in from outlying parts of the country, and meetings were being held from the verandas of the main saloons. Some blue-shirted soldiers were trying to organize things, and frontiersmen were being led away in squads for issue with army equipment and drilling. Then a battery of field guns came racing down the main street, their outriders shouting at the top of their lungs to clear a way for them.

Careless said drily: 'Looks like you're expectin' a war, colonel.'

The colonel said grimly: 'We have a war on our hands. The Comanches have come ridin' down from the hills. There isn't a white settlement in the next eighty miles that hasn't been burnt to the ground by them red devils.'

And then quickly he lifted his grey eyes to meet the equally grey eyes of the big, drawling Texan. The colonel said sourly: 'What in heck's name am I tellin' you this for?' He stamped back to his chair behind the table. He was growling: 'As if you wouldn't know! As if Careless O'Connor wouldn't know more than we do!'

But for all the growling manner in which he spoke, there was no hostility. The colonel clearly had a respect for his big visitor.

The big visitor promptly ambled into the old freight station, hooked a chair into position with his spurred boot, and then settled himself with his feet on the table. He looked comfortable. He looked as if any moment he might go to sleep.

The colonel nodded grimly, and yet there was amusement in his eyes as he looked at that trail-stained, torn and tattered-shirted Texan. He said sarcastically: 'Go right ahead, Careless. Just make yourself at home. I'm only the commanding officer of this area, in charge of an Injun war.'

Careless tipped his hat to the back of his head. He puffed good-naturedly on his pipe and waited until the colonel had finished. Even then he waited until the colonel asked him his business.

'What's brought you up here?' The colonel tried not to show his interest. He knew that O'Connor was a frontier agent of the United States Federal Bureau, and he knew that he hadn't suddenly appeared in this district without very strong cause.

Careless blew smoke towards the ceiling. He said: 'I'm looking for a gun.'

The colonel's eyes widened. 'A gun?' His voice was incredulous.

'Sure, a gun. A big gun. A cannon, some people would call it.' His head gestured to where more artillery rumbled down the noisy, busy sunlit street of this cow-town. 'Bigger than them,' he added.

The colonel leaned forward, his eyes narrowed. 'You're not askin' after the Santa Anna cannon, are you?'

The laziness left those grey eyes immediately. Careless brought his feet to the ground. 'Does that mean that someone else has been askin' after it?'

The colonel scratched his thinning hair in perplexity. 'Now, what in Hades is there about that gun to bring people all this way, askin' questions?' he rumbled. 'Sure, there's been other people here askin' about the Santa Anna cannon. Now you come along. Careless, you tell me, what is there about that gun to make you come all this way to look for it?'

Careless was no slouch with his brain. He neatly evaded the question by asking others. He said: 'I want you to tell me all you know about the Santa Anna cannon. And I want to know about these guys who have been here before me, askin' questions.'

The colonel found himself answering that frontier agent as he might a superior officer.

14

He looked out on to the dusty street of this township of Running Squaw, now right on the edge of the Indian war. He said: 'It's sixty miles west of here, at a settlement called Rattlesnake on the river of that name. The place was one of the first to be overrun by the Comanches when they came down from the hills. I guess it's just a pile of ashes now.'

'And the Santa Anna cannon?'

'I guess that's lyin' among the ashes, too.' The colonel withdrew his gaze from the hot, dusty street and looked into the narrowed, grey eyes of the big Texan opposite. 'It was no good, though, even before they burnt the town.'

'It was spiked?'

'It was spiked by the artillery officer before they withdrew from the town. The artillery never let their guns get intact into the hands of an enemy!'

'I'm not concerned about the gun being intact or not,' said the big *hombre* softly. 'I just want to know where it is and the quickest means of gettin' there.'

'You mean you're plannin' on ridin' through Injun territory with this war on?' The colonel looked at big Careless as if he couldn't believe his ears.

Careless knocked his pipe out on his heel. 'I reckon to,' he said lightly. 'I guess I'll make out. I've always done so before.'

The colonel seemed to draw in a deep breath

at that, as if he didn't altogether share the casual giant's confidence. 'OK, big fellar! If that's the way it is, I'll try to help you.' He was just busting with curiosity to know what powerful reason made a frontier agent anxious to ride sixty miles through hostile territory for the sake of a cannon that was no use to anyone.

But aloud, he said: 'I think you should meet Major Abigay. He was the officer at Rattlesnake when the Comanches attacked the town. He was the officer who spiked the gun before leaving.'

Careless looked interested. He said: 'That's a bit of luck! I'd like to meet him – now!'

And that last word was something like an order. A second later the colonel realized that he was jumping to it like any ordinary soldier in his command, and for a second, being human, he felt vexed.

But he sent a man for Major Abigay, and then he tried his best to pump the big Texan about that mysterious cannon.

Watching narrowly, he said: 'It's got quite a history, that gun.'

Careless was cutting up some tobacco again. 'It sure has,' he said agreeably. 'It was made for Napoleon's army in Europe, but he kinda lost it when he went fightin' the Dook of Wellington in Spain. Then the Spaniards shipped it out to Mexico when they thought to bring their king into the western hemisphere.'

'Only it didn't stay in Mexico?'

'Nope!' Those big hands rubbed the leaf into fine shreds. 'When the United States went to war with Mexico, the gun got captured. It was the Mexican dictator's prize gun, so they always said. A mighty good gun, considerin' its age. Santa Anna used it to wipe out his prisoners for an afternoon's sport, so they told us.'

'But Santa Anna, that Mexican dictator, he's gone now?'

'He's gone. I was there when he went.' Careless O'Connor had been in many wars, including the Mexican one. 'The gun got carried back through New Mexico as a prize by some American filibusters. They got it up the river as far as Rattlesnake, then they couldn't float it any futher. So they fixed it, thinking it would be of use in case of Injun warfare.'

The colonel shook his head. 'Rifles – repeaters, at that – are the guns for Injun warfare. Injuns don't mass enough for field-gun fire, and they don't get scared of the shot any more.'

Careless nodded agreement. Then there was a silence between them. If the colonel had hoped that this preamble would cause the Texan to betray his mission inadvertently, he was disappointed. That Texan had told him nothing he didn't know.

'Here's Major Abigay now,' the colonel said, as a shadow fell into the room.

Careless turned in his chair, just lighting his pipe again. Through the wreathing smoke he saw a tall, lean, hard-bitten artillery officer. He saw a thin-face that was blackened almost to the colour of an Indian's. He saw eyes that were narrowed and sharp, and seeming to be hostile even now, without cause for hostility.

The major saluted, and his salute was somehow reluctant. Plainly he wasn't a man who liked to have to acknowledge anyone else's superiority. Careless O'Connor, sitting there, had the feeling that he was in the presence of a ruthless, self-opinionated man. The kind of man who thought more of himself than of others.

The colonel said: 'Major, this is O'Connor, generally known, for good reasons, as Careless.'

There was a little grin on his face as he said it. He was realizing, like other men, that he didn't even know O'Connor's first name. He got a look of warning from O'Connor then, and didn't explain O'Connor's complete identity. Careless had suddenly decided that he wouldn't immediately make his position as Federal frontier agent known to this lean, hard-looking major.

He never knew why. It was just a hunch, but he acted on it. O'Connor had lived as long as he had because he had learned to work upon hunches.

The colonel went on, 'O'Connor's interested in that Santa Anna gun you were manning out at Rattlesnake, major. He figgers on goin' out there to take a look at it.'

The colonel didn't even know what Careless wanted with that gun, and he looked towards the big Texan for further explanation. O'Connor didn't give it.

The major had turned, and he seemed to be crouching slightly as he faced the sprawling frontier agent. Those eyes that looked down at O'Connor were mean and glinting and slitted. There was something curiously menacing about the major as he faced the Texan.

'What do you want with the Santa Anna gun?'

O'Connor looked up at him levelly, not intimidated by the harsh question or the manner of the speaker. 'Information,' he said laconically.

The major seemed to glare at him. 'What information?'

O'Connor got to his feet. It was deliberate, as if he were rising to be on level terms with this man who appeared to want to browbeat him.

'Tell me what happened to that gun. Tell me the best way to get through enemy country to Rattlesnake,' he ordered.

The major licked his lips. 'We bust that gun before we left the place; it's no good to anyone. What's your interest in a gun that's no good to anyone?'

O'Connor said, 'That's my business, brother.'

The major snapped angrily. 'Major to you! Don't you realize you're speaking to an officer of the United States Army?'

O'Connor's grey eyes looked up and down that stiff, tense figure. Humour crept into them. He said: 'I'd be blind if I didn't.'

Then he turned his back contemptuously upon the major. The colonel hadn't attempted to interfere. He knew that O'Connor could hold his own with any army officer.

O'Connor jerked his head towards the major. 'This galoot kinda flies off the handle somewhat, colonel. Mebbe you'll tell him to quit bein' on his dignity and give me the information I want.'

The colonel looked at that angry major and said, 'I'll do something even better, Careless. The major will take a party of cavalry and provide escort for you into Indian territory.'

He lifted his hand quickly as the major seemed about to interrupt. 'No, I don't mean right up to Rattlesnake. But I figger that if you can get over the Horn Mountains, you'll have a good start on your journey. The major can return once he's seen you through the pass.'

Major Abigay must have realized then that the big Texan was no ordinary frontiersman. His eyes looked smoulderingly angry at the colonel, but he said nothing. O'Connor looked round quickly and caught an expression in those hard, grey eyes. He saw that Abigay was thinking deeply, and he suddenly thought, 'This guy's got somethin' on his mind. I'd better watch the fellar.'

20

The colonel said, 'The last bit of information you'll want, Careless, is about those other *hombres* who were interested in the Santa Anna gun. They rode in yesterday. You'll find 'em down at one of the saloons, I reckon.'

O'Connor was already moving towards the door. He said: 'How many?'

The colonel said: 'Five of them. An' they're tough. Mighty tough, Careless.' His eyes fell to the twin guns in the wellworn holsters round Careless' narrow waist. 'I reckon you'll need those guns when you meet up with 'em, Careless.'

Careless went out into the sunshine. As he went through that door he said, 'I'll be back. Have the escort ready to ride out with me in a couple of hours, Major.'

Major Abigay gazed after that big form. He was in a temper. He didn't like the way this rough-neck civilian gave orders – and expected them to be carried out.

His eyes switched round to the colonel's. He failed to notice the amusement on the older man's face. 'Who does he think he is?'

The colonel told him then. 'He's the biggest trouble-buster in the employ of the Federal Government. He's a frontier agent, and he's only sent on mighty important jobs.'

The major saluted. 'I'll get a party to ride out with O'Connor, then.' He went out quickly into the sunshine.

21

He saw O'Connor kick upon the batwings of a saloon down the street, and the major's head seemed to lower and come forward, like a rattlesnake's in that moment before it strikes.

The eyes of the major were fiercely hostile. For he liked being a major, and he knew that if O'Connor got through and found that gun he wouldn't retain his cherished rank. Instead, he would be discharged with disgrace from the Army.

For he had permitted a serviceable gun to fall into the hands of an enemy, and had gained promotion by declaring otherwise.

TWO

MARKED MAN

O'Connor went from saloon to saloon, looking for five men. He found them at length. They were standing drinking beside full packs that had obviously been put together for a long trail ahead. Instinctively, O'Connor knew them to be his quarry when his eyes alighted upon them.

He pushed his way towards them. Everywhere men were drinking noisily, excited by the events of the past weeks, and by the activity of the moment.

O'Connor listened to the loud laughter that spoke of nerves, and heard the boastful voices of near-drunkards – and knew that to be a sign of nerves, too. He didn't blame any man for feeling jumpy at the thought of meeting the Comanche nation. The Indians were bold and fearless fighters, and they wouldn't be driven back except after

23

the most ferocious of battles.

But his interest wasn't in battles. He was interested in these five men who had been asking questions about the Santa Anna cannon. He was puzzled. He wanted to know who they were and what their interest was in a cannon that was no longer of any use to anyone.

He got his drink and stood close up among the five men. After a few seconds he decided that one of them was a Mexican. The other four had the cut of Border adventurers. He saw them, slip-waisted, with guns tied down in the manner of men who practised the swift draw.

They weren't doing much talking. But Careless did get one or two muttered sentences. They didn't seem in a good mood.

He heard one rannie growl, 'The heck, it would have to happen! There isn't a thing we can do until they drive them blamed Injuns back beyond the Rattlesnake River.'

Another growled back. 'That might mean hangin' around here for weeks. I don't like hangin' around any place.'

There was a silence, while the men drank and thought. Then yet another rannie said uneasily, 'If we hang around here they'll expect us to join the Volunteers. I don't aim to be in any man's army. I figger we should try to get round the Injuns, and make for Rattlesnake from the south.'

They were a morose group of disgruntled-looking rannies. Big Careless was inconspicuous, standing close to them. They would never have realized his interest, but someone deliberately told them.

Careless heard a harsh, loud voice addressing him. 'Looks like everyone's kinda interested in that Santa Anna gun, O'Connor!'

Careless came round slowly, his grey eyes in his big flat, battered face very hard. They met the glinting, malevolent eyes of the major. He realized that the major had deliberately followed him in, and had spoken loudly in order to attract the attention of these five *hombres*.

The five drinkers had turned at once and were looking at the army officer and the big, untidy frontiersman. Their eyes were quick with suspicion now, and their hands were poised above the well-worn butts of their too-handy guns. O'Connor saw the professional crouch, and knew that suspicion had made them ready to throw lead.

Careless squared up to that major. He said, coldly and dispassionately: 'You did your level best to tip the men off that I had an interest in the Santa Anna gun. Major, mebbe you haven't done your uniform any good with that!'

The major's eyes blazed. He didn't like civilians who talked back to him, not even civilians who held positions with the Federal Government. And yet there was a touch of malicious triumph in those grey, glinting eyes.

Because he knew he had succeeded. He knew that those rannies, crouching back of the broad-shouldered Texan, had marked O'Connor down as an enemy.

O'Connor said: 'Why did you do it?'

The major ignored the question. He said: 'I don't reckon to have any men ready for you in two hours time, O'Connor. My men have been workin' all day, drillin' the militia. It isn't right they should be sent off at two hours' notice.'

O'Connor's head came round to look at those five silent gunmen. He was doing some quick thinking. He nodded slowly. 'OK, major, it's as you wish. We'll start with first light tomorrow.'

The major almost blinked. He hadn't expected O'Connor to give in so easily. He looked suspiciously at the big, broad-shouldered man and an uneasy thought crept into his mind. 'He's up to something!'

O'Connor deliberately shoved his way through those five *hombres* and got himself another drink at the bar. That done he turned, his hat shoved back from his brown, perspiring face, and leaned with his elbows on the bar while he took a drink. His eyes surveyed each of the quintet in turn.

They looked at him, hostility written on their faces. Then one of them said 'C'mon!' He jerked his head and the other four followed him out of the saloon. Evidently they didn't intend to get talking with the frontier agent.

O'Connor looked at the firewater in his glass. He was thinking: 'Mebbe they've seen service in Mexico. Mebbe they know something about that li'l gun. Mebbe they know who I am, and what I'm up here for now.'

He went out to his horse and rode it down a street that was difficult to negotiate because of the commandeered wagons, that were going to be used as baggage trucks for the army. Some were ox-drawn, and they were the worst, because they moved so slowly and took up the entire street as they came through.

Down the street a hundred yards he saw someone sitting on a roll of blankets. It was a girl, though she was almost disguised by the customary Western dress of jeans and fringed buckskin shirt. She was dark-haired, blue-eyed, and she had a face that was as brightly intelligent as it was pretty. O'Connor drew rein alongside her.

She looked up at him, and her eyes didn't run away from his. He touched his hat – that disgraceful old ruin – in salute.

She said briskly: 'On your way, cowboy! My father told me never to speak to strange men.'

O'Connor's eyes glinted good-humouredly. He eased himself forward in his saddle, and drawled: 'I reckon your paw sure had something when he told you that.'

The girl sprawled back comfortably on her blanket roll and waited for him to go. He didn't go. He said, quite politely: 'I figgered you'd mebbe tell me where I could find a room and bed for tonight, ma'am.'

She relaxed at that question. Plainly the big, rough-looking frontiersman wasn't trying to make up to her. She shrugged. 'I wouldn't know. I don't live here.' And then she threw in for good measure: 'You're a lucky guy to have the money to get yourself a room.'

'You're as flat broke as that, huh?'

She nodded. She didn't look sorry for herself. He said: 'Haven't you got folk around here who'll help you?' These tough cow-towns were no places for young girls to be on their own.

She said confidently: 'I'll get by, mister. I reckon something'll turn up.'

O'Connor lifted his head, and his eyes looked round him. He saw the inevitable loungers on the board sidewalk, and he knew they were watching this girl like hungry-eyed wolves.

He said: 'Sure, I guess something will turn up.'

He didn't say any more, but clicked with his tongue, and that sent the horse walking away down the main street again. The girl looked indignant. She wasn't used to men just walking away from her like that.

Big Careless was thinking as he rode down the street: 'Sure, that gal can look after herself. But no gal can stand up to some of these varmints once they get their minds set on something. They've got plenty pisen in 'em, I reckon!'

He made a few more inquiries, and then found a house run by the inevitable widow – always there was some woman who had lost her man in the Indian wars and in consequence was reduced to taking in boarders. She talked a lot, but her house was clean and her price wasn't bad, considering the times.

He went up the stairs and looked at the little room with its narrow cot in one corner. He said: 'It'll do.'

They came on to the dark landing together, and he was pulling out some Mexican silver dollars that were good currency in Arizona. He said: 'You got any more rooms to let?'

She shook her head. 'I reckon my house is as full as can be. I got people sleeping everywhere.'

He rattled the silver coins in his hand thoughtfully, and then said: 'I figger you could fix a hard-sleeping guy like me somewhere, even if it's in the kitchen.'

She was beginning to look indignant, and then surprise came to her face. She said: 'Aren't you goin' to sleep in that bed yourself?'

He sighed and shoved back that sweat-stained hat, and she saw his nose was wrinkling as if he was thinking hard and found it difficult. Then he said: 'Nope! There's a gal stranded down the road

SECRET OF THE CANNON

on a blanket roll. I figger that gal will be a mite safer in your house tonight, ma'am, than sitting in the street.'

His eyes met the widow's. 'You go out and fetch her in, ma'am. She's just down the road a piece. Tell her you've got a bed for her, but don't tell her I'm paying for it.'

The hardness went from that middle-aged woman's face at that. 'You know the gal?'

'Never met her before in my life.' He shook his head. 'An' I'm ridin' west to-morrow, ma'am, so don't think I'm tryin' to spark the gal.'

She wiped her hands vigorously and unnecessarily on her apron. 'It's mighty kind of you, mister,' she said. 'Mebbe I can be a mite generous myself. I'll fix you with a good big chair, and you can sleep by the kitchen fire tonight.'

Careless grinned and patted her on her shoulder. 'The minute I saw you, I said: "There's a woman with a mighty big heart".'

The widow became severe again. 'On your way with you, you blarneying Irishman!' she said.

But she liked the little bit of badinage all the same.

Careless went out to his horse and took it round to a livery stable. As he rode away, he saw the widow woman speaking to the girl, sprawling on her blanket roll, and the widow woman was pointing towards her house up the street.

Careless came in with the other boarders for

supper around nine that night. The lamp had been lit in the parlour, a parlour that was also the dining-room. It seemed that at least half-a-dozen men were putting up there for the night, and they nodded when big Careless lounged into the room and took a seat at the rough plank table. The food was plain, but it was good. Careless looked up in surprise.

The girl who had been sitting on her blanket roll was serving food to the men. Careless looked over the heads of his companions and met the eyes of the widow woman perspiring over her fire in the kitchen.

She turned away and went quickly on with her work. The girl came and served Careless, and as she put the food before him she looked at him as if he were a stranger – as if she had never seen him before in her life.

Careless thought: 'That's for walking away from her instead of hangin' around like all them other wolves.'

Her coldness towards him didn't upset the big Texan. He ate a hearty meal and enjoyed it. Then he ambled into the kitchen and put his feet up alongside the stove. The widow woman was removing the remains of the meal. Then the girl came bustling in, and when she saw the big, lounging figure in the comfortable chair that was to be his bed that night, she neatly knocked his feet down and brought him sitting upright in his seat.

She said coldly: 'Outside, cowboy! This is no place for big, idle fellows like you.'

And she drove him out of the kitchen.

The widow woman turned, her brow contracting angrily as she saw the treatment accorded the man whose generosity had provided this girl with a safe bedroom for the night. She was about to say something when she caught the wink of the genial giant as docilely he went out of the kitchen ahead of the girl.

All the same the widow woman tried to put in a good word for Careless. He heard her say: 'You don't need to get so uppity, Jane Frazer. I reckon sometime it looks mighty comfortable to see a man enjoyin' hissel' in a woman's kitchen.'

Jane Frazer said determinedly: 'I aim to earn that bed you so kindly offered me, Mrs Thomson. And I figger I can work a whole lot better without lazy, lounging men in the place.'

Careless chuckled and went out into the dark night. He was thinking: 'That's the way it is, is it?' The girl thought she was working to pay for her bed . . .

Within a quarter of an hour of leaving that boarding-house, Careless knew he was a marked man. He knew that before the night was up he'd have lead shot at him.

THREE

BLACKMAIL

He went into the Two Gun Saloon and five hard-faced rannies stopped talking and drinking the moment he entered. As he stood at the bar he could feel their mean eyes drilling into him.

He went on to another saloon. After a few minutes they drifted in. Deliberately he passed on to the Silver Dollar Saloon, with its gaudy drapings and tinny piano and 'live' show. And after a few minutes five cold-eyed gunmen came walking in through the batwings.

Careless decided to enjoy himself after that. He went from one saloon to another, and led them a dance. Sometimes he ducked quickly out through backdoors so that all the time he kept his trailers on edge, and they couldn't have enjoyed their night's work.

Finally they must have realized that he was just

fooling with them, and they quit being trackers. They just failed to turn up at one saloon, and Careless, swilling the drink round in his small glass, tried to figure out their next move.

When he'd stayed up long enough he set off to go back to the boarding-house. The moon was slanting down, throwing the buildings opposite into a deep shade. It was a shadow dark enough to hide a hundred enemies, and yet Careless walked confidently, sure that he knew where he would find his men when he came up to them.

He'd got it all worked out. There was an alley right opposite the widow woman's boarding-house. It was on the shadowy side of the street, and it led out on to the prairie. It meant that an ambush could be contrived, and then there was plenty of room for escape for the perpetrators.

He lit his pipe down the street, and he knew that in the momentary glow from his match they would have recognized him. He didn't let the light stay on long, however, because that might have invited a rifle bullet. He stood where he was, puffing hard at his pipe until a hot coal glowed redly. Then he walked across to that side of the street that was black with shadow.

Those men sitting their horses quietly in that narrow alley had seen the glow on big Careless O'Connor's face. One whispered tightly: 'There's the guy we want! We've got to put him right out of the race now. O'Connor's got too big a reputation to be allowed to live!'

They had their Colts out, half-raised to cover the approach of the man crossing on to the shadowy sidewalk of this main street.

They couldn't see him because of that blackness, but they knew he was approaching because, like a solitary red eye, they could see that glowing coal in O'Connor's pipe.

Five pairs of guns lifted and levelled all in one direction. They fixed on a place about eighteen inches below that advancing pipe. When a man had a chest as big as O'Connor, that was the target to aim for. You couldn't miss at twenty yards!

When O'Connor was right on the edge of the alley, the spokesman for the quintet whispered: 'Now!'

Ten guns blasted away all sleep for people around that alley. Shattering waves of sound echoed and re-echoed between the clapboard buildings.

They were only twenty yards from O'Connor, and they were deadly marksmen. Yet they missed him by a yard!

O'Connor had walked down that sidewalk holding his glowing pipe rigidly out at armslength from him. Ten shots had damaged a lot of air three feet away to his right, and that was all.

The pipe was stuffed into his pocket in one

lightning move. That pipe was a favourite of O'Connor's, and not even for five gunmen was he going to drop it. Then in one incredibly swift movement his heavy Colts came leaping into his hands, flaming orange-yellow in the shadows and hurling lead towards his opponents.

But they, too, got away unscathed. The sudden roar of those .45s had terrified their horses. They were bucking and rearing and wheeling in mad confusion, getting in each other's way. It saved the riders, because O'Connor couldn't train his guns on them.

But one shot from Careless' Colts bit through a taut rein, and as the horse flung its head backwards and almost sat on its haunches, the rider was hurled into the dust.

His horse scrambled to its feet and set off at a mad clatter, straight towards where O'Connor was standing at the corner of the alley and the main street. Its rider promptly grabbed the stirrup of a companion and went running out with his four comrades into the darkness of the prairie.

Careless saw that horse leaping madly towards him. He seemed to sway to one side, scarcely giving ground at all as it bore down upon him. Then, just as it came level, in a beautifully expert manner he seemed to fall against the horse's side, and in the same movement roll on to its back. A fraction of a second later and he was in the saddle and his feet had found stirrups – his hands

grabbed the broken reins by the bit and pulled
back . . . and that horse was under control before
it had run half the length of the main street.

Even a horse knew better than to fight against
the strength in those mighty arms.

O'Connor turned the trembling, sweating
beast and walked it back to the livery stable. He
put it alongside his own, unsaddling it and
rubbing it down, talking and making friends with
it until it was soothed and he knew it would sleep
and be a useful animal for the following day.

Then he went into the widow woman's kitchen.
There was a queer smell following him, and he
couldn't understand it, and he didn't like it. It
even came into the kitchen with him.

Then he heard a sound, and he came wheeling, his hands instinctively going to the butts of
his guns.

He relaxed. Jane Frazer walked in. She avoided
his eyes, and said: 'Coffee?'

He looked at her, and then realized that the
coffee-pot was on the stove, as if waiting for his
return. He said, nodding: 'Coffee.'

He sat down. His eyes were speculating. She
poured out the coffee, still not looking his way.
When she came to sugar it, she asked: 'Sugar?'

'Some.'

His eyes widened. She put in so much sugar
that she could almost have stood the spoon
straight upright in the cup afterwards. He said

admiringly: 'Gee, I must be the favourite son tonight!'

She pushed the coffee into his hands. Her face was flaming red, and still she couldn't meet his eyes. He was thinking again there was a goldarned awful smell hanging around his clothes, and he didn't like it.

He heard her say, in a very small voice: 'I got the truth out of Mrs Thomson.'

'The truth?'

'About my room. It was very nice of you.' Her eyes did look into his now, and they were grateful and yet ashamed. 'You were so kind, and I didn't know it, and I was not nice to you.'

Careless was beginning to feel all hot. And it wasn't anything to do with the girl. And that smell!

But he said, 'Oh, and why weren't you nice to me?'

She didn't answer but instead pushed the plate of food across to him.

An expression of agony crept over Careless' face. At the same moment the girl's eyes widened with alarm. She exclaimed, 'Something's on fire!'

Careless leapt to his feet with a howl of pain. 'You're goldarned right there is!' he exclaimed.

Frantically he was putting his hands into his jeans pocket. He dragged out the smouldering lining – and his old, charred pipe. The stink of burning cloth filled the kitchen.

Careless crushed out the creeping red glow, then looked ruefully at the useless pocket. 'I sure forgot my pipe was lit when I stuck it into my pocket,' he said ruefully.

'You must have been very absent-minded to have done that,' the girl said, smiling. She had very pretty blue eyes when she smiled, Careless was noticing.

He agreed. 'I guess I had something on my mind when I did it.'

He ate heartily of the supper she had provided, and when he'd drunk that coffee she was ready with another cup for him.

She said, 'You're not sleeping in that chair tonight!'

Careless merely stretched his long limbs and settled down in the comfortable seat. 'You try to dig me out of here,' he invited, a lazy grin on his big brown face. 'You're sleepin' in that bed tonight, Jane, so quit arguin'.'

She shrugged; she knew she was beaten. She started to thank him yet again, but neatly the big man diverted her conversation. He said: 'How come you're here in Runnin' Squaw?'

Her eyes dropped at that, and he knew she was brooding over the recent past.

'I was in Rattlesnake when the Comanches came and captured it. The men got us away across the river. We rode two-up for days, with the Comanches all the time riding after us. Every

39

settlement we came to was burnt over our heads by the Indians and we had to continue our trek east.'

He murmured, 'It must have been a bad time.'

'They were bad. They got worse when we were about twenty miles from Running Squaw.'

Careless cocked an eye interrogatively. She explained. 'Our horses gave out. We had to walk the rest of the way. And I hate walking!'

They both laughed. Careless could understand her feelings. He, too, had been born to the saddle, and he didn't go much for walking, either. He didn't press her with questions, because he had a feeling she had lost a lot – perhaps her nearest relatives – in that battle at Rattlesnake.

Suddenly his eyes jerked wide as he heard from those soft red lips the words – 'Santa Anna.'

He heard her murmur, 'Who was Santa Anna, Careless?'

'Why do you want to know?'

She fiddled with the fringe on her buckskin shirt before answering, and he wasn't sure that she was quite open in what she was saying now. 'Oh, it's just that we had a gun at the settlement. It was a very big, very heavy gun, and we all thought it was going to be protection for the town in case of attack by Indians.

'When the United States Army got to know we had this big gun they sent a detachment of soldiers to man it. They were going to make Rattlesnake a frontier fortress in time. However, the Comanches attacked before any plans could be made effective.'

He reminded her gently, 'Where does Santa Anna come into the story?' though he knew well enough.

Her hands fluttered again to the fringe of her shirt. 'I was forgetting.' She laughed, but rather too quickly. 'It was silly of me. Of course, you wouldn't know, but that gun was said to have been Santa Anna's own favourite cannon. It was a beautiful gun. It was highly ornamented, and yet the artillery officer said it was one of the best guns he had ever fired.'

'You mean Major Abigay?'

She nodded. Suddenly he was alert. There was a curious brooding intensity in her eyes at the mention of Abigay's name.

'He was a lieutenant in those days.'

Her eyes lifted to meet Careless'. She said, 'If there's a man in this world I hate and mistrust it's Major Abigay. Don't have anything to do with him if you ever run across his path, Careless!' So intense was her emotion that, without realising what she was doing, she had put her hand on his sleeve and was gripping him tightly. Careless looked into those blue eyes, and now, suddenly they were blazing with anger.

He rose. He said, 'What do you know agen

Abigay?' Because what the girl said fitted in with his theories of the man.

She sighed. Then she shook her head. 'Either I'm mistaken or he's done a terrible thing,' she whispered, but she wouldn't say any more than that.

So big Careless put his arm round her slim young shoulders and steered her out into the hallway. 'It's time pretty gals got some sleep,' he smiled. 'An' if pretty gals don't need sleep I know one guy who does. I'm hittin' the trail early in the mornin'.'

He stood at the foot of the steps, and her hand clasped his where it rested on the plain wooden rail that guarded the stairs. Her eyes were very soft as she looked at the big man, and the lamplight gleamed in the dark coils of her soft hair. She looked very desirable in the lamp-light.

'I'll never forget your kindness, Careless. Secretly I was scared stiff of the thought of sitting out there on my bedroll all night. I'm sorry you're leaving, but I'll be up to see you off.'

He smiled and patted the hand. 'Don't you thank me too much. I reckon Mrs Thomson's goin' to tell me to keep my money tomorrow. She looks mighty stern, but she's got a great big, tender heart underneath. So you don't need to thank me. Instead, tell me what you'd like most of all in this world.'

She answered promptly, 'A horse!'

Careless nodded. 'Just wish hard enough before you go to sleep, an' mebbe there'll be a fine roan standin' out in the street waitin' for you by sun up.'

Careless was right in his prophecy about the widow woman. When, next morning, he tried to pay her, she refused the money. She said, coldly, sternly, 'You didn't sleep in the bed, did you? Then why should I take your money for it?'

Careless sighed, still holding out the silver dollars. 'I slept in your kitchen chair, didn't I?'

'Pah! No one charges a man for sleeping in a chair.' Mrs Thomson looked more stern than ever. Careless chuckled and slipped his arm round her plump waist and gave it a squeeze. He said, 'You can't kid me, Mrs Thomson. I figger you're a mighty fine woman, and if I ever get back this way, lordy be, I'll be a-sparkin' you!'

Mrs Thomson exclaimed, 'Away with you, you blarneying Irishman!' But she was pleased. She made Careless the best breakfast he'd had in years – or so he told her.

Jane walked round with him to the livery stable when he went to get his horse. She was still grateful to him. Overnight the big, drawling Texan had become a hero to her, and there were times when there was a light suspiciously like adoration in her lovely blue eyes when she looked at him.

Careless whispered to the straw-chewing old

43

man who ran the livery stable, and money changed hands. Then Careless swung into his saddle and prepared to ride away to find his escort. He leaned down, hat in hand as he said goodbye to the girl.

She said wistfully, 'We may never meet again, Careless.'

Careless nodded. 'That's the way it often is out West,' he said. There was some regret in his own eyes, though he was used to parting now. She was a lovely girl, and no healthy male likes to ride out on a lovely girl.

He rode away. Jane started to walk back to the boarding-house, her head drooping a little, as if she didn't like parting with the big Texan who had so quickly seemed to be a lifelong friend. When she was halfway to Mrs Thomson's she realized that someone was following her.

She turned. It was the old man from the livery stable. He was leading a roan ready saddled and bridled for the trail.

He said to her politely, 'You go on, ma'am. I'll follow with your hoss.'

'My horse?' She stared in surprise at the roan. It was quite a good-looking beast. 'Aren't you making a mistake? That isn't my horse!'

The livery man started to spit, then remembered he was in the presence of a lady and restrained himself. 'Begging your pardon, ma'am, but this is your hoss. It's bin your hoss for the last ten minutes.'

Enlightenment came to the girl. 'You mean that Careless—'

'Mr O'Connor left a message. He said, "You sure must have wished mighty hard last night. This is yours from now on". That's what he said. A mighty fine fellar, Mr O'Connor,' ended the livery man.

It was a dazed girl who took possession of the horse. Dazed, but now that she had it, her mind was racing round to the possibilities it opened out to her. As she walked into that boarding-house her mouth was hard, and in her eyes was a steely determination.

There was a lot about Jane Frazer that was mystifying.

Careless found his escort awaiting him outside the Wells Fargo office. There were six troopers and Major Abigay. The major was in a bad temper.

Careless greeted him: 'Good-mornin' Major. You all ready?'

The major didn't wish him any good morning. Instead he rapped, 'Not quite. There's still one man to come.'

With that he turned on his heels, leaving his horse in charge of one of the troopers, and he went striding down the main street.

O'Connor looked good-humouredly towards the trooper holding that horse. He said, 'He didn't sleep well last night. What's bitin' him?'

The red-faced cavalryman grinned. There was something about the big casual-looking Texan that warmed the hearts of most rough-and-ready men like the trooper. He said, 'We're waitin' on a sergeant. He's from the artillery, an' the major particularly wants him along. He's had one argument with the colonel about it already.'

Careless looked after that lean, angry figure and his eyes were thoughtful. He had a feeling that Major Abigay never did anything without good reason.

He went inside to see the colonel. The officer was ready for the trail. He smiled as Careless ambled in.

'Good news, Careless. The Injuns are massing north of Three Pines. We're goin' out to meet 'em, an I reckon I've got enough men to give 'em the darndest hiding the Comanches ever had. By tonight they'll be streamin' back to the hills.'

'If they're not?'

The colonel looked sobered by the thought. 'If they lick us, there won't be any Running Squaw by tonight. An' the Comanches will be through into Arapho territory. Together they'll drive on until they reach the Mississippi, by the look of things. They've got blood in their eyes, an' we've sure got to stop 'em.'

Careless was looking on to a sun-warmed main street that was a scene of almost frantic activity.

Troop after troop of militia were riding through the town on their way towards Three Pines. Baggage wagons were trundling along, filled with food, medical supplies and ammunition.

The colonel spoke shortly, as if suddenly he remembered something. 'I had trouble with Major Abigay. I wanted him to take a cavalry sergeant with you, but he became insistent about taking an artillery sergeant with him. I needed artillerymen, but he would have his way.'

He seemed angry with himself, like a man who had yielded, though his better judgment was against yielding.

Careless said, 'I heard about it. I don't see why he needed an artilleryman. They don't sit hosses like the cavalry.' Then he said, 'I'll go out an' try to find Abigay. I want to be well into Indian territory before you rout them Injuns.'

Careless went walking round the wooden buildings that formed this little cowtown. It didn't take him long to find Major Abigay. As he turned a corner he saw two blue-uniformed figures ahead of him. There was something in their manner that brought him to a swift halt.

A short, squat sergeant was speaking to Abigay, and there was something in his manner which wasn't usual between sergeant and superior officer.

Careless heard a rough, angry voice say, 'I've got to settle my debts afore I leave Runnin'

Squaw. I need a coupla hundred bucks, an' I'm goin' to have 'em!'

Major Abigay's face was black with fury at being addressed in this manner. Careless expected to see him strike the man down, his rage was so great.

But instead, to the watching Texan's surprise, Major Abigay pulled out some money and slapped it into the sergeant's hand.

Careless turned and walked back to the Well's Fargo office. He was very thoughtful. When he ambled up he found the major already there.

Careless squinted up at the lean, scowling major and demanded; 'Waal, are we ready?'

The major said shortly, 'We'll be ready just when I say so, O'Connor. I'm in charge of this party. I'm waitin' for a man to turn up – an artillery sergeant who knows the back trails better than any of us.'

Careless didn't say anything at that. Instead he seated himself in the shade and prepared to wait. Twenty minutes later the sergeant came walking up. His manner was truculent.

The major merely said, 'Get mounted, Sergeant Holbein.' Then, his eyes switched across to the comfortable giant, seeming half-asleep in the shade. 'I'm ready to move now, O'Connor,' he rapped.

O'Connor walked across to his horse. When he got near to where Holbein was trying to find a stirrup for his foot, his eyes lifted suddenly and looked at the blue-chinned, squat-bodied sergeant. Careless thought, 'He's spent some of them dollars on firewater!'

They struck south from the town to keep well away from the troops, riding in a dust cloud across the arid mesquite. They rode for an hour, and then Careless moved up alongside the major and began to speak with him.

'This Sergeant Holbein,' he began. 'Was he part of your gun team on the Santa Anna cannon?'

Major Abigay grunted. Then he said, with every appearance of reluctance, 'Yep. Why?'

Careless shrugged. He said deliberately, 'Why is he blackmailing you, major?'

The major dragged on the bit of his horse so savagely that it nearly toppled backwards in pain. When Careless looked into the major's eyes there was murder in them. Then he saw the major's hand swinging savagely towards him, and there was a carbine in it, plucked from its saddle-holster.

Careless jerked back in his saddle, but that swinging butt crashed towards his head.

FOUR

NIGHT MARCHERS!

Careless acted like lightning. As he went back in his saddle, his mighty arm swept up and round, and he deflected that murderous blow with the brass-bound butt as if it were a fly being brushed away.

Major Abigay almost toppled out of his saddle under the impetus of that blow, and big Careless completed the disaster for him. The Texan grabbed that rifle in the same movement and jerked – and Major Abigay came crashing down on to the mesquite. His horse skittered and began to prance away, and two cavalrymen detached themselves and came riding out to round it up.

Careless looked down upon the fallen officer. The man's hat had come off and he didn't look as an officer should, there on his hands and knees in the dust. The man's eyes were murderous, but they didn't hurt the big *hombre* sitting that ungainly brute of a horse.

Careless said, 'So he is blackmailing you. The way you behaved kinda shows that hunch to be correct.' His eyes looked contemptuously at the officer who was swaying to his feet. 'What sort of a hold has a sergeant got over an officer of field rank?'

Abigay just growled through set teeth, 'There's a limit to what I'll stand from you. Give me that rifle!'

O'Connor slapped it back at him quickly, and Abigay hadn't expected to get it so easily, and he muffed it and hurt his fingers and it dropped into the dust and added to his discomfiture.

Careless said coldly, 'You won't do a thing to me, major.' His eyes worked round to the sergeant and the cavalry who had closed in about them, awaiting their superior officer's command. He said, 'You started that, and you didn't come so well out of it. Try gettin' in my hair agen, an' see how far it gets you next time!'

He pulled his horse round at that, in itself an action of contempt as he turned his back upon the man standing down there in the mesquite. He began to ride westwards towards the Horn Mountains.

After the faintest of hesitations, as if temper might get the better of him, Abigay turned and got on to his horse and rode after O'Connor. The men fell in behind.

When they were riding level again, Abigay snarled at the frontier agent, 'Next time I get in your hair, O'Connor, I won't get out of it!'

The big, flat, brown face came round to look at him. For the first time Abigay saw the muscles that built up that strong, fighting-man's face and he wondered that he hadn't noticed them before. The trouble was, this big *hombre* deceived everyone by his apparent casualness, his air of lazy unconcern. He realized now that it was a pose, that it was the velvet that covered the iron fist.

O'Connor was an iron man through and through, Abigay thought.

Careless just said one thing more. 'I figure you don't want me to reach that Santa Anna cannon either, major. An' that sure makes me wonder why!'

Then it was Careless' turn to drop back, leaving a sullen, smouldering-tempered Abigay to lead the way into the wooded defiles that climbed towards the pass through the Horn Mountains.

Careless was watching the country carefully, his eyes flitting from cover to cover in their eternal quest for a lurking enemy. All the same, he manoeuvred so that he came alongside that blue-chinned artillery sergeant who sat his horse like a sailor.

He shot a glance at Sergeant Clay Holbein. The man was feeling the heat now, because it came on top of too much alcohol in the past twelve hours. His eyes were nearly gummed together, and beads of sweat stood out on his red, mottled face.

O'Connor said, softly, 'I figure you ain't enjoyin' this ride much, sergeant.'

Little, mean eyes that were filled with dirt came round to embrace the big Texan. A growling, bad-tempered voice said, 'That ain't my fault. I figure I'd have done better to have stopped back in town or gone with the rest of the artillery northwards.' His head jerked towards the northern skyline, as if to indicate whereabout the colonel's army would be riding now.

O'Connor was quick to seize his opportunity. He said, 'Why did the major insist upon your comin' with us, sergeant? This is a job for a cavalry unit.'

The sergeant opened his mouth to say something, and there was malice and cunning in those little eyes as they looked at O'Connor – it was as if they said, 'Don't I know things about that major that'd startle you!'

Then the major had turned in his saddle and seen them talking together and his lean face grew black with passion immediately, and he bellowed, 'Quit that talkin' back there! An' you keep away from the soldiers, O'Connor!'

O'Connor just grinned and spurred up so that he rode in the major's dust. It was evident that Major Abigay wasn't going to let him wheedle any truths out of the sergeant.

An hour later, when they were riding along a game trail that passed through undulating, bush-covered territory, ideal for an ambush, they heard the first sounds of battle roll down to them ten miles from the north. There was a faint, prolonged booming sound. Involuntarily all reined at once and quietened their horses and sat their saddles, listening.

One of the troopers muttered, 'Them's the big guns. I figure the militia have met up with them blamed red varmints!'

There was more sullen booming, and it came to them in little eddying waves of sound. Unmistakably now the battle had begun up at Three Pines.

Major Abigay's harsh voice was heard to exclaim, 'Waal, that's to your advantage, O'Connor. I reckon our boys'll be keeping the Comanches occupied, an' that'll give you a chance to slip through to the Rattlesnake River.' His manner suggested he wasn't so pleased that it was going to be so easy for the frontier agent.

The major pulled his horse round to send it riding up a short steep incline. And then he dragged upon the bit and pulled his horse to a sudden halt.

For he found himself staring at the war-painted face of an Indian!

The Indian was as surprised as the officer. He

had just appeared over the brow of that tiny hill, and they could see only his head and neck and the ears of his horse. Then the Comanche screamed a terrifying war-cry, and at once that ridge became alive with warpainted Comanche warriors.

O'Connor was shouting immediately, 'Into that defile!'

He almost bundled those troopers into the mouth of a narrow, rocky gorge just off the game trail. Major Abigay came hurtling in on his mount, alighting at top speed and crashing behind cover with his carbine ready for action.

They all came off their mounts at the run, and dived for cover, leaving their horses to trot into the shelter of that valley. Out from the dark greenery of that bushy hillside leapt Indian horsemen. O'Connor realized that by sheer bad luck they had run into a strong body of Comanches apparently heading to join the main army. In all, there must have been two or three dozen of them, coming hell-for-leather down that slope towards them.

He saw dust rising, saw the wild gleaming eyes of hard-pressed ponies – saw the wide-open mouths of paint-daubed Indians in their feathered plumes. His Sharps seven-shot repeater sighted and fired. A rider came crashing off his mount. Another rider went down, and then the troopers opened up with their carbines.

That sent the Indians pulling madly away. There was a pause while the Indians grouped in the distance, and O'Connor knew that another charge would be attempted within minutes.

Abigay called to him. 'O'Connor, you get forward to where them rocks are. You've got a repeater, an' you'll be more useful out there.'

O'Connor's brown face puckered questioningly as he peered over a boulder towards the rocks indicated. The Indians were still circling in the distance. O'Connor looked across at that long lean officer, sprawling a dozen yards away to his right. He called, 'I don't see any good in goin' out there. I can shoot just as good from this position.'

The major lost his temper, 'I told you I was in charge of this party! I give orders, O'Connor. Go over there as I tell you!'

Just then the Indians broke up and formed into a long line, and came charging madly towards the mouth of that little defile. They came in screaming their war cries, and the way they raced it was obvious they meant to finish off this wandering band of palefaces in a matter of seconds.

It was a savage fight. The Indians crashed right in among the white men. To those men lying prone behind the defences it seemed suddenly as though they were under a cascade of horseflesh and naked, whooping Indians.

Careless came leaping to his feet, the empty Sharps rifle dropping to the ground as his hands clawed for the butts of his heavy six-shooters. He saw rearing ponies, exulting Indians leaning from their saddles to strike down at the defenders. Then, fighting for his life, his guns boomed out.

Another revolver joined in. It was the major's.

It was those three revolvers which turned the scales in favour of the white men. The Indians couldn't stand up to the rapid fire of those deadly, short-range guns. Copper-hued forms tumbled everywhere as the shots rang out. They stood it for a few seconds, striving madly to bear down upon the two men with those flaming revolvers, but they were driven back.

Inevitably there came a time when one lost heart altogether and pulled his pony out of the fight and fled. That gave the other Comanches their lead and they went after him.

A dozen dead Indians lay in among those rocks. Another eight or nine were crawling away, hurt and for the moment out of action.

The defenders hadn't escaped. Two men had been lanced or struck down by war clubs. Two others had been wounded but could still carry rifles.

Careless wiped away the sweat from his brow, and as the dust settled he said to that lean, panting major, 'That sure was a warm moment, major.'

Abigay didn't answer him. His eyes were looking towards that artillery sergeant. Holbein was leaning on his rifle and looking morose.

Abigay's eyes went round now, looking for the dozen or so Indians who had got away. He saw their plumes over distant bushes and he said, 'I reckon them varmints don't intend to let us get away with this victory.'

Careless nodded. He knew the vengeful nature of Indians on the war trail. They wouldn't want to return to their main party with a story of defeat at the hands of a tiny group of white men. He thought, 'They'll lie up in them bushes, an' when we quit this cover they'll try to down us with their arrows.'

The silent arrow was a deadly missile in country with cover as good as this.

Abigay said again, 'You, O'Connor, get out there among them rocks.'

The big Texan looked at the dust at his feet. He began to charge up that stinking old pipe of his. Then he lifted his head and looked that major squarely in the eyes and said, 'Like heck, I'll go out there in front of your gun, major!'

He didn't say any more than that, but he stood in the attitude of a man challenging another. Major Abigay's face blackened with fury. He raged at his orders being flouted, but also he knew that Careless had seen through his manoeuvre.

Abruptly Abigay turned away. Careless took considerable precautions after that to keep behind the major's gun. He didn't want to be the central figure in an 'accident.' For he knew that was in Abigay's mind.

Abigay had wanted to put him out there in front of the defenders, with the plain intention of shooting him from behind when opportunity presented. His men would never know that he had fallen to a bullet from the major's gun and not by attack from the Indians.

Late that afternoon, when there were no more sounds of battle from the far north, one of the cavalrymen who had got himself raised on a rock shelf above his fellows, called down, 'There's someone on a hoss gallopin' a half-mile to the south of us!'

That brought them all rearing up behind their defences. After a while that lone rider came nearer, crossing no more than a quarter of a mile away. Then they all saw that red horse and its small rider.

The moment Careless saw the pair his pipe dropped from his mouth. He exclaimed, 'By glory, I know that hoss!'

It was the roan he had presented to Jane Frazer that morning – and if that wasn't Jane Frazer riding into enemy country, he was a son of a Dutchman!

Then Careless' eye became diverted by a movement away to his right. He had a momentary impression of someone riding away from them through the thick scrub and he knew what that meant.

He exclaimed: 'The Injuns have seen that gal! Some of them have taken off after her!'

He began to run back into the arroyo to find his horse. It came trotting up when he ran into the cool, shady valley, whistling. He mounted at the run, swinging up as lithely as a rodeo expert.

Abigay came running across from where he'd been with the wounded. He was shouting angrily, 'Where are you goin'? Who told you you could ride out' on us?'

Careless got impatient and roared, 'I'm goin' after that gal, what d'you think?'

He didn't give the angry officer a chance to say anything more, for he went racing past so quickly, that the major had to throw up his arms to shield his face from the stones kicked up by those flying hoofs.

O'Connor knew what risks he took in leaving the safety of that little party. He knew there would be Indians still left watching the soldiers, and he knew he had to ride right through the cordon if he were to get on the trail of the girl. But that didn't deter him. He lay flat on the back of his horse, his face almost hidden by the flying black mane. His Sharps was reloaded and held to his thigh with one hand that was so big it made the rifle look like a toy.

All at once as his horse came leaping over the brush, he saw Indians rising in his path. They were converging on him, all on foot but nonetheless dangerous for all that. They leapt towards him, shouting exultantly, thinking that in his ignorance he had ridden in among them.

Then that rifle boomed, and an Indian fell back out of the fight. Careless got in another shot, but missed because his horse shied away with the first explosion. Then Careless was hacking his way through the leaping copper-hued forms. He parried blows with his rifle and then struck out ferociously and knocked opponents away from his horse's head before they could grab the bridle.

Then he was through and away – not quite. A Comanche had grabbed the tail of his horse and was hanging on. The horse was alarmed and beginning to circle and rear, and that was giving the other Comanches time to run up again.

Careless tossed the rifle round and caught it by the foresight, and in the same movement he flung himself along the back of his horse, sweeping out with the rifle butt. The Indian was knocked away, and Careless' horse went plunging forward instantly.

Careless raised himself and turned in the saddle and fired until his rifle was empty. Anything to keep those Indians down among the cover and away from where their ponies were hobbled in a nearby grove of beeches!

When his Sharps was empty he sat round and reloaded as he forced his gallant beast south-westwards to cut across the track of that fleeing girl. He was climbing again, beginning to rise out of the trees and brushwood. Another few miles and they would be above the tree line and exposed on the bare mountainside.

He began to see the cleft through the mountainous range – the pass by which he had intended to cross over into Rattlesnake County. It was evident that the girl was heading that way, too.

As he crouched along the extended neck of his flying horse, Careless wondered what madness had brought her so far away from the safety of Running Squaw.

Then he wondered if in fact Running Squaw was safe. He wondered if the militia under the army officers had managed to defeat the Comanche Nation.

He stopped speculating. Three Indians were riding through the brush ahead. He saw their bobbing plumes, and the war-paint that adorned their faces and naked bodies. In some way he had managed to ride level with them without coming on to their heels, but now they had seen him and it was a race between them as to who should get second to that roan climbing the bare hillside in the distance.

Careless' giant horse won that race. But it won because Careless had a fine rifle and was an accurate marksman even on the unsteady back

62

of a galloping horse.

As the three war-painted Indians tried to close in on him, he let fly with that Sharps, and he must have been very close, because they pulled away and galloped parallel with him.

Twice again they tried sudden rushes to get in at him, and each time he drove them off. Two of them, he knew, he had wounded in those charges.

Then he heard sounds behind him, and when he turned he realized that other Indians had come in pursuit of him. He faced five or six Indians now, though two of them he'd already wounded.

He got out on to that old wagon trail that the girl was following. He was only a few miles from that narrow gap that gave between the mountains. But his horse was labouring now. The girl had disappeared through the defile.

When his labouring horse reached the pass, Careless leaped down out of the saddle and let the beast walk on. He knew it wouldn't go far.

Deliberately he squatted on the bare open trail at the mouth of the high-walled narrow gorge that led through the Horn Mountains. He sat there and pointed his Sharps rifle towards those mounted, painted Indians.

There must have been the impulse in those warlike Comanches to ride down this solitary paleface, but by now they had learned to respect that quick-firing rifle that he carried. They knew that if they charged, some if not all of them must die before they reached him. They adopted other tactics.

Very occasionally he glimpsed a feather or the flick of a moccasin as an Indian moved from one cover to another. He saw them gradually close in on him, and yet he went on squatting there.

For every moment that he held back these Comanches gave Jane a chance to get a lead on her pursuers.

Suddenly Careless realized that one of the Comanches had got within arrowshot of him. He caught a glimpse of a form rising quickly and stringing an arrow to a short bow and sending it, hurling it towards him all in one swift, practised movement.

Careless went flat on his back at that to evade the arrow, and his rifle jumped as he fired it.

Neither hit. The arrow smashed itself on the bare rock behind Careless, and his bullet chipped the bow out of that warrior's hands. Careless was on his feet immediately. Then very casually he started to saunter back into the pass now.

Two hundred yards inside, driving his horse before him as he walked, he turned and once again squatted on the trail. The Indians had risen from cover. Now all over again they had to start their laborious approach towards him behind rocky cover. When they were again within bowshot range, Careless rose to his feet and once again tramped a couple of hundred yards down that sheer-walled pass.

His tactics infuriated the Indians. After that first arrow, he never once let them get within bowshot range of him. All the time night was coming on. The girl was heading farther and farther away from these Indians. And his own horse was resting and would be ready to take the trail again.

There came a time when Careless knew he had outwitted his enemies. This time when he rose he walked over to his horse and swung himself lithely into the saddle. He saluted the furious Indians ironically, and then sent his horse galloping along the trail. He knew there'd be no pursuit worth talking about. For those Indians had to run back well over a quarter of a mile in order to get their own ponies, and that gave him all the start he needed.

His eyes sought the trail. Many horses had ridden along it, and for a time he was unable to pick up the tracks of the girl's roan.

Then he saw recent tracks where a solitary horseman had left the trail in order to cut off a wide bend. He started after it.

After a while those tracks ran into other tracks, and he wondered whose they could be. For these appeared to be shod horses, and therefore not Indians'. They were recent and were heading westward. Careless reined and looked down on them, and thought a long time.

After a while he decided there were five in the party, and he could think of only five white men who might be sufficiently interested to head for Rattlesnake while an Indian war raged over the country.

His eyes were grim as he looked at the dying sun over the plain before him. He thought: 'Havin' to wait for that darned sergeant this morning gave that Mex and his pards chance to get out of town ahead of me!'

He knew she was alone, though; that she hadn't joined up with the five Border adventurers. For her horse's tracks were laid on top of the earlier ones.

He followed her trail down that mountain side without once seeing her. When darkness came he unrolled his blanket and went comfortably to sleep in a patch of brush so dry that he would have heard anyone – even an Indian – trying to steal up on him.

Next morning he mounted after only the briefest of meals, and took up the trail again. Late in that afternoon he found the girl.

He topped a rise in country that was fairly wooded. He had a superb view of the great plain beyond that stretched as far as the Rattlesnake River. In the far distance he saw a rider – the girl.

She was sitting her horse in an open space near

to which were the charred ruins of some unfortunate settler's homestead.

He saw her studying some object that looked blue from that distance, but he couldn't guess what it was.

Then his attention became diverted by another sight. He saw movement in the trees behind the girl. Into his mind flashed the immediate thought, 'Indians!'

Five horsemen rode out from the brushwood and encircled the girl.

They weren't Indians. He couldn't identify them from that distance, but he was willing to bet they were that Mexican and the four gunmen whom he had seen in the saloon bar back in Running Squaw. They seemed to speak for a few minutes, and then suddenly there was activity.

It seemed as if the girl tried to ride away, but immediately those men came spurring round her. Careless just managed to make out their actions. One grabbed the roan's head. Another caught the girl and held her.

After a few more minutes while their horses milled around together the six riders began to head westwards again towards the Rattlesnake River. Careless dug his heels into the sides of his horse and sent it plunging down on to the plain below. His face was grim. Those men weren't the kind to have hold of a girl like Jane Frazer.

He lay low along the neck of his horse, while its

drumming hoofs kicked up a shower of dirt and a cloud of grey-yellow dust. He took risks, going short ways that were rough and treacherous, but he had to catch up with that party before he lost sight of them.

Suddenly he found himself thundering down towards that open space that had been cleared by the settler. He got the smell of charred wood in his nostrils, and he looked at the blackened ruin of a farmhouse with interest as he rode by.

Suddenly he drew rein. Lying on the ground ahead of him were several corpses. Some were Indians; one wasn't.

He thought: 'This is where the settlers made a fight with the Comanches when they started to burn up the country.'

Some of the Indians hadn't lived through that battle. Neither had an American soldier.

Careless rode across to that blue-uniformed body. He looked down from his saddle upon it. The man was sprawling on his face. There was blood dried black upon his neck. Careless looked again and saw that he was an artilleryman.

Then he pulled his horse's head round and went thundering along the trail after the girl. Now he kept seeing that party, and he began to ride with greater caution. He followed them for an hour, winding in and among the clumps of trees that dotted this fertile plain. Night began to approach, and he saw obvious signs of the men looking for a camping place.

He drew rein and watched from a distance. He saw them ride into an arroyo and dismount. That would be a safe place for white men to rest in this hostile territory.

Careless dismounted, too. He led his horse into some thorn scrub and tied it to a tree stump. Then he began to walk stealthily towards that arroyo.

As he approached he got the smell of burning wood in his nostrils and he realized that they had lit a fire.

It took Careless until almost darkness before he reached the mouth of that arroyo. Then he lifted his head cautiously and realized that he was almost on top of the look-out man. The Mexican was sitting with his back to a rock, watching out over the plain. He looked to be half-asleep, as if he didn't think there was likely to be any danger, and he was taking it easy.

Suddenly that Mexican saw a mountain-sized form rear from a bush no more than six feet away, and come diving headfirst towards him.

That Mexican never got a chance to alert his comrades. A mighty, crushing weight descended upon him, and in that same instant hands like vices gripped him and immobilized him.

He opened his mouth to cry out a warning but, so quickly that it dazed him, he was twisted on to his face and his head gripped between two powerful legs that effectually stifled any sound from his mouth. He wasn't a weakling, that hardy Mexican Border adventurer, but he was like a puny child in the hands of that giant.

His arms were gripped painfully behind his back, and then, in spite of his resistance, each hand was shoved in turn through the tight belt that the Mexican wore. Then Careless ripped off the man's neckerchief and tore off the hem. He neatly looped the Mexican's two thumbs together and then, as the desperate, stifling man struggled and kicked, Careless caught a flying boot and pulled it towards him so that the heel rested on the Mexican's belt and the toe was neatly caught between the fastened thumbs.

That Mexican wasn't going to get out of those simple bonds very easily. In fact, he wasn't going to get out of them at all unaided!

Careless fixed the rest of that torn neckerchief around the Mexican's mouth, gagging him. Then he took his weight off the man and silently rose in the gathering darkness and prepared to enter the arroyo.

It was right at that moment, before he was actually inside the arroyo, that Careless heard Jane begin to scream. There was terror in her voice, and the big Texan's hair seemed to lift on his scalp at the sound of it. He couldn't bear to hear a woman or child in fear, and its effect upon him sent him leaping furiously into the darkened arroyo.

He turned a bend in the tiny valley. There was a fire, a small red one glowing, and in the background he saw horses. But it was the scene around the fire that enraged him.

In the firelight he saw Jane struggling in the grip of a woolly-chapped gunman.

She was fighting furiously to release herself, and he was laughing unpleasantly, for he knew she couldn't get away.

The other men were squatting round the fire, watching with interest. Careless saw those faces, made ugly by the sneers upon them. There was no mercy in their hearts for this defenceless girl; no thoughts of going to help her.

Careless covered the intervening distance with gigantic bounds. A startled quartet of gunmen suddenly saw a giant form looming out of the shadows. They hadn't time to move before he was upon them.

Careless jumped straight into the fire and kicked out with both feet. Burning brands rocketed towards the trio squatting around the fire. They flung up their hands to protect their faces, and went reeling back, and that was just how Careless wanted it.

In that second, before they had a chance to recover and go for their guns, Careless had grabbed the woolly-chapped gunman by the back of his neck. He had a hand that hurt when he gripped. Just now it hurt so much, that gunman thought his neck was going to break and he let go of the girl and tried frantically to tear that hand away from its grip.

Careless, enraged at sight of a girl being badly treated, gripped the gunman by the seat of his pants with his other hand, and then that gunman found himself being hoisted into the air by a display of enormous strength. He was hurled on to his comrades, who were just rising to their feet and drawing on their guns.

When they'd sorted themselves out from that assault, they found themselves staring into the blue eyes of twin Colt guns. Back of those guns was a big, bulky shape, whose face they couldn't see, but whose identity they knew at once.

Jane had jumped to his side with a glad cry when she recognized him. She was holding his arm, and was clinging so close to him that he knew then what fright had been in her mind this past half-hour or so.

He stood back of his guns and his voice leapt out like the lash of a whip at those four *hombres*. 'If you've harmed this gal I'll sure put lead into your worthless carcases!' he growled. But Jane gripped his arm the tighter and said, 'They didn't hurt me. You were in time. Don't start any gunplay, Careless.' Her pleading voice reduced the anger in his mind, and his mood changed.

He said, 'Get your hoss, Jane. We're ridin' out.' Then he added, 'Bring their hosses with you!'

At that, in spite of the threat of his guns, the gunmen leapt forward in furious protest. 'You can't leave us without horses in Injun territory!' one man exclaimed.

That was the law of the West. You never left a man without horse in enemy country. It was as good as signing his death warrant, and the equivalent of murder in most men's eyes.

Careless growled, 'I don't intend to leave you without hosses. But I reckon you don't deserve any charity.' He jerked his head behind him. 'You'll find your hosses tied back among some thorn scrub a few hundred yards away. I'm takin' 'em so's to keep you from followin' hard after us.'

Jane had mounted, and now she went out of the arroyo, leading their five beasts. Careless started to go back, crouching as he did so. At the bend in the arroyo he suddenly whirled and went leaping after those trotting horses and came vaulting into the saddle of one from behind. It reared in surprise, but he fought it down and kicked it into speed.

He called to the girl, dimly seen in that darkness, 'Keep ridin'. Let's get out o' range o' them varmints.'

Within a few seconds Careless had spotted that thorn scrub, and in that time the gunmen hadn't opened fire. Probably they were afraid they might attract attention of wandering Indians if they fired. Careless thought they must have discovered their Mexican companion and were by now releasing him.

True to his word, the big frontier agent carefully tied those horses to the thorns. Then he mounted his own ungainly but powerful beast. Taking the girl's bridle, he walked westward for a good half-hour.

It was eerie work, because they blundered into shadowy masses that were painful thorns. And it seemed to them there were lurking forms in the blackness, as of Indians about to spring on them.

Jane was frankly terrified.

Once she whispered, 'It's worse than when we came east!'

Then at least they had had a party of considerable numbers.

Careless didn't answer. He was peering ahead. A moon was clearing the trees behind them. Silver rays began to give them light.

They were looking down a valley that was crowded with shapes. And some of the shapes were moving.

Careless reined in and his rifle jumped to his shoulder. For within forty yards of them came the head of a ghostly procession, a column of mounted Indians that must have been a quarter of a mile long.

FIVE

ADDED DANGER

They had to stand there and let that procession trail wearily by. They daren't move in case movement brought attention upon themselves. They sat their horses within view of those Indian warriors, and no one came riding from the ranks to give them a closer inspection.

Careless licked his lips and thought, 'They must figger we're part of their army, standin' aside to rest our horses.' He prayed they would go on thinking that.

It seemed an eternity before the last of the Indians rode along the valley bottom and was finally swallowed up by the night. Then both released their breath, as if they had been holding it these last ten minutes.

Jane's awed whisper reached his ears, 'We were so near, yet they never saw us.'

'They weren't expectin' to see white folk, I reckon.'

He put out his hand. Jane caught it. She was trembling. It was ten minutes before she had recovered from that agonizing moment. Then they went on. Careless said, 'Looks like the Comanches got a bad lickin'.' Clearly that was a defeated Indian army that had ridden by.

They rode for another mile or two helped now by that moon, and then Careless said he thought it would be safe if they camped for the night. He picked a place where giant rocks broke out of the arid soil and kept off the sighing night wind.

They had two blankets with them, and that was enough. Within a few minutes both were rolled up and asleep.

The big man had the girl out of her blanket before dawn. They were mounted and riding westward before the first rays of the yellow, Arizona sun came to dispel the night's chill.

Jane was tired and would have lingered on in sleep, but she knew Careless was right when he said they had to keep moving – they had to keep ahead of those five mean Border adventurers.

They rode for two hours and then, when the heat of the day and the dust of the trail made life unendurable, they halted by a bubbling stream in a rocky basin and, climbing down stiffly, made a brief but welcome breakfast. Careless didn't risk lighting a fire, but there was plenty of water and that was sufficient.

They left their horses down at the water and climbed to the top of the hill to the north of the basin. It gave them a magnificent view of all the surrounding country.

After cautiously looking all around them, Careless relaxed. He said, 'I figure we're well ahead of pursuit.'

Perhaps the Border adventurers were following by sign, and that was a pretty slow way of progressing. Careless thought they could stay there a good hour before continuing to the Rattlesnake River only another fifteen miles ahead of them.

They lay together comfortably in the shade of some bushes, and their eyes watched always for sign of movement over the shrub-covered land on all sides.

Careless finally said, 'I sure got a shock when I saw you ridin' through that Injun pack.'

Jane smiled at him. She had recovered her nerve now, and looked composed and very attractive. She said, 'I got a shock, too, Careless. I suddenly found myself being chased by Indians!'

Careless didn't tell her what had knocked those Indians out of the race. There were other things he wanted to know. The first was – 'What made you start to ride westwards? You know it isn't healthy bein' anywhere in this land with the Comanches on the war-trail.'

She nodded. Her eyes had lost their laughter.

There was a brooding look about them, as if they had become tinged with bitterness. She didn't answer him for a good minute, but Careless was content to wait. He knew she would open up to him in time.

She did. She said, 'It's that man, Major Abigay.'

It startled him and brought him sitting up quickly. 'What about Abigay?'

Her eyes sought his and there was horror in them now. 'You didn't see—' she began to whisper.

Careless' thoughts flashed suddenly to that blackened ruin in the clearing, where he had seen her standing over the body of that dead artilleryman.

He said quickly, 'Mebbe I did see. You're thinkin' about that soldier who's lying dead back there.' His head nodded the way they had come.

She whispered, 'Yes . . . him. Careless, did you see the way he had died?'

Careless remembered the blood congealed on his neck. 'I figure he got shot from behind.'

Jane whispered, 'Major Abigay shot him!'

'Abigay!' He was incredulous. She saw his grey eyes widen as he turned to look at her. 'But why? How did it happen?'

Now his eyes never left her face as she told him the story of that nightmare trek back east.

It was a story of desperate situations, of constant skirmishes with eager, scalp-hungry Comanches.

The men had formed a rear party to beat back the constant attacks of the Indians, and one by one they had fallen. But all the time they were managing to get farther eastwards, towards the promised safety of some strong settlement.

'I was riding behind a soldier,' Jane told him. 'We were a very weary party of people when finally we rode into Whitesides. That's the settlement we came through yesterday.'

He knew she was referring to that burnt-out homestead, and he knew she was coming to the point of her story. His eyes abruptly switched to a dust-haze that rose miles to the east of them.

'A lot of people had ridden in from the surrounding country, and we thought we'd be able to rest and perhaps make a stand against the Comanches. But it wasn't to turn out like that.

'Scouts came in to say that the Indians were pouring like a red flood across the Rattlesnake River. They advised against any stand being made. They said we were bound to be surrounded and eventually massacred.

'So wearily we got back on to our horses to resume our trek, and the settlers who had come to Whitesides went to get their animals to follow us.'

Careless saw her hand lift to brush back a tendril of hair which blew about her face. He could feel her emotion now, remembering those horrifying moments.

'We were just out on the back trail, when all at once Indians seemed to spring out of the ground, coming from nowhere. At once our men went diving for cover. My soldier companion jumped off the horse and slapped it to get it to take me out of danger. He was a very good young man, that soldier.'

Her lips were trembling. She was thinking they were all brave men, because always they had fought to protect the women and the weaker ones in their party and give them a chance of their lives – at a cost of their own.

Jane's eyes came round to meet Careless'. 'There's something I haven't told you yet. All the time I was riding with that soldier he was muttering angry threats against Abigay. He seemed infuriated with the man, and Abigay, I'm sure, knew it. Once the artilleryman growled to me, 'I won't keep my mouth shut when we reach Runnin' Squaw.' I saw that soldier go running back to find cover to make a stand against those screaming, war-whooping braves. Then I saw him fall to the ground, dead.

'I never saw an Indian with a gun,' Jane told Careless earnestly. 'The only gunfire was from our own party. Yet when that soldier went sprawling on his face I didn't see any arrows sticking out of him. I did hear a carbine fire just to my right. I remember looking that way and I saw Abigay with his gun to his shoulder.'

Careless said, 'Mebbe he was firin' at the Injuns.'

Jane nodded. 'That's why I kept my mouth shut. It's a serious matter to accuse an army officer of the murder of one of his men, and I'd never have suspected such a thing but for those words of that soldier just before his death – that he was going to open his mouth about Major Abigay when he got into Running Squaw.'

Careless' eyes again roamed the horizon. Then they became riveted upon something that moved several miles east of them. He watched intently. Horsemen were breaking through the brush toward them. He didn't move, all the same. He was comfortable and wanted to hear the end of the story.

Jane was sitting erect, gripped by the tides of her emotion.

'When I got to Running Squaw I didn't know what to do. I couldn't accuse Abigay, but I felt that I couldn't go on in life holding that suspicion and not doing anything about it.

'So when you gave me that horse I made up my mind what I would do. I thought it would be safe to make a day's ride towards Whitesides, in view of the fact the militia were going out to meet the Comanches in battle. I set off with the intention of finding that soldier's body in order to see for certain how he had come by his death. Did you see what I saw?'

Careless' voice was harsh. 'I saw a man dead from a bullet wound in the back of his neck. That's what I saw.' His grey eyes swung away from those two advancing horsemen, and looked at Jane. 'An' you say them Injuns didn't carry firearms!'

She shook her head. She said, 'What do we do now?'

Careless said grimly, 'We face Major Abigay with his crime!' His brown forefinger stabbed out towards the advancing horsemen. 'He's comin' towards us now!'

The girl was startled. She followed the direction of his pointing finger. She could just make out two blue figures riding towards them.

Careless said grimly, 'I reckon Major Abigay sure wants to make certain of riddin' the world of me!'

Abigay must have sent back the cavalry with their wounded, but he had taken up relentless pursuit himself with the artillery sergeant.

Careless thought, 'Mebbe that's what the sergeant's got to blackmail Abigay with.' He voiced his suspicions to the girl, and then was surprised to see her shake her head.

'No. I remember Sergeant Holbein was still in Whitesides getting the other people out. Only I saw that incident.'

Careless looked at her and said, 'Don't let Abigay know what you suspect.'

'Why?'

'Because Abigay's not the kind of man to trouble over such things as sex. Bein' a gal won't protect you from a man of his calibre.'

Careless rose and helped the girl to her feet. He was saying, 'I don't like the look of that dust cloud east of us.' And then his eyes became riveted upon more movement within half a mile of where Abigay and the sergeant came walking their horses towards them.

He saw more horsemen. Then he saw a sombrero – and knew the identity of that quintet.

Careless said, 'C'mon, Jane, let's get movin'!'

He took the girl down the slope at a run. Their horses were refreshed now and ready for further action.

Careless hoisted the girl into her saddle. He was going to ask her what the Border adventurers had said when they recognized the beast, but he reserved the question until later. Just now he wanted to put distance between himself and those advancing men.

Because, although he didn't tell Jane, not only were the Border adventurers and the two army men approaching, but also a mighty horde of Indians!

SIX

THE GUN!

They swung out westwards again, and as they galloped steadily across the mesquite Careless thought about those approaching Indians.

He thought they were probably a rearguard who had stayed behind to hold back the militia while the main mass of Comanches streamed westwards in defeat.

This was going to make things awkward for them. For the logical place for all to cross the Rattlesnake River was at the settlement which had been built on a ford.

Careless didn't get worried, all the same. He'd found that worrying didn't help in any situation.

Instead he spoke about the roan.

The girl laughed, 'When Dave saw me with his horse—'

'Dave?'

'One of those five men who captured me yesterday. Dave was the one in woolly chaps. When he saw me riding the roan he nearly threw a fit. He got mighty angry with me, and called me' – she mimicked – 'a durned hoss thief!'

She laughed again, but then her voice seemed to catch a little. 'Perhaps that made him more unpleasant towards me than the others. You came just as he was beginning to get nasty.'

Careless didn't bother to explain how he'd got the horse.

The girl kept questioning him about riding westward.

At first Careless said, with plenty of truth, 'Jane, goin' this way is just as healthy as any other. To turn now would be to run slap-bang into a whole lot of enemies.'

Later he told her that he wanted to go to Rattlesnake because he wanted to look at a gun that was there.

'The Santa Anna cannon?' The girl was surprised. Then she said, 'A lot of people seem interested in that gun.'

'A lot of people?'

Jane replied, 'I remember when the filibusters brought it up river from Mexico as a prize. Almost immediately afterwards a man came riding in to Rattlesnake offering to buy the gun. He said he was a collector of army ordnance.'

'The settlement wouldn't sell it?'

'No.' She shook her head. 'The settlers reck-oned it was more useful as a weapon against Indian attack than in some eastern museum.

'Then, later, another man came riding in and offered an even larger sum of money for the gun. This time there was no chance of the settlers sell-ing it, even though the amount offered was an astonishing sum. The army had announced that it was sending men to take over that gun, and he had to go away empty-handed.'

Careless, jogging by her side, asked abruptly, 'Did you ever hear the name of Reiffel mentioned in those negotiations?'

She shook her head. 'I never heard it, though, of course, I didn't actually hear anything of the negotiating. Why?'

Careless shrugged and said nothing. He was riding with caution because there was no knowing what bodies of Indians were lying up within the shelter of the clumps of trees and bushes they passed. Shrewdly, Jane Frazer said, 'That gun must be worth a lot for all this interest. What is so valuable about it, Careless?'

He grinned. 'You wait an' find out!'

When they were within sight of the trees that bordered the winding Rattlesnake River, they ran across recent tracks of Indian ponies. At once Careless swung north so that there was no danger of running on to the party.

It brought them out a mile above the burnt-out settlement of Rattlesnake, and Careless was faced with the dilemma of riding down to the easily negotiable ford or of trying to swim the river.

And the trouble was a ford was a good place for men to rest up ... a mighty fine place for an ambush, Careless was thinking.

He told the girl, 'Looks like we'd better swim the river. Are you game?'

She was game. For answer she simply rode her sweat-stained roan into the water and started it for the western bank.

It was not a pleasant crossing. The river looked narrow until they began to swim it. Then it seemed the widest, most open river they had ever known. They felt conspicuous, slowly battering against a current intent on sweeping them down to the ford, and they couldn't help feeling that all the time eyes were watching them from the greenery on either bank.

It was with relief that they finally rode their dripping horses out of the water and sent them clambering into the cover of some cottonwoods.

Careless reined in. It was always as well to give a horse rest, because if it came to a race for life everything might depend upon the stamina of a man's mount.

As he sat on his horse he was listening. There was no sound save for the birds which occasion-ally fluttered in the shade of those overhanging trees. Finally he decided it was safe to go through the vegetation towards the settlement.

Suddenly they broke out of the foliage on the edge of the open space which surrounded the settlement. They looked at it from a distance. It was a blackened ruin, with charred palisade stakes that still remained upright but were no longer of value as a defence. Within were blackened frames of huts, with charred beams still presenting the outline of the buildings that had been there until the fire. It looked a black, dead place, with those gaunt ribs sticking up out of the ashes.

It made Jane want to cry, because it had been home to her. It brought memories to her of the people who had lived there and who had died on the trek back east.

But Careless wasn't getting sentimental. He was watching for movement within the settlement. None came. All the same he sat there a good quarter of an hour, watching, before giving the order to ride up to the place.

They approached cautiously, Careless with his Sharps ready and the girl holding a gun across her saddle bow.

But there was no movement from within the palisade. They rode through the gate that had been opened by those Comanches to let in their mounted brethren. Inside was a scene of devastation, with corpses still lying where they had fallen. They rode slowly into the middle of the settlement.

Careless was looking everywhere. He said, 'Jane, where's that Santa Anna cannon?'

She pointed to a blackened shell that had once been a log hut. 'It was mounted on the roof of that building.'

She stayed where she was while Careless rode towards that collapsed hut. She watched him circle it, looking intently among the ruins. Then he pulled his horse round and came spurring back to her.

She found herself asking, 'Well, are you satisfied?'

His eyes were looking towards the western hills. He shook his head. He said, 'That gun isn't there. Someone beat us to it an' got it away somehow!'

Jane was startled. Then she realized that this big, comfortable-looking frontier agent didn't seem vastly perturbed. She said, 'Is this disappointing?'

He shook his head. 'Nope. Mebbe it's just as well. That fire might have damaged it. I reckon them Injuns took the gun down afore burnin' the hut it was built on.'

She asked, 'Why?'

He shrugged. 'I reckon to find that out pronto.'

He was riding towards that blackened gate that still hung from the charred palisade. She started to come after him. He told her, 'No, Jane. I figure you're as safe here as anywhere. I'm goin' a piece along the trail. That cannon, by all accounts, was a mighty heavy piece of equipment. I figure it hasn't been taken far, an' I intend to find out who took it and why.'

She stayed where she was, watching him as he spurred quickly across the open ground towards the shelter of those distant trees. Then she dismounted, and walked her horse back among the buildings. She was taking it down to the water to drink, when suddenly she dragged it hastily back behind the charred stumps of a log hut.

Someone had ridden out on to the eastern bank of the river.

It was a man wearing a sombrero.

Careless rode with caution. Truly this side of Rattlesnake River was enemy teritory. There was no knowing how many Indians were back across this side of the river now. He wouldn't last long if he ran into any, he knew.

All the same he had come so far and he wasn't going to turn back without knowing what had happened to the Santa Anna cannon.

The cannon had been carried by hand. These Indians, of course, wouldn't have any sort of mechanical facilities, not even a freight wagon. They must have lifted it on a litter of strong poles, and carried it in stages along the trail.

His sharp, knowing eyes read the signs in the dust as if it were a book telling him the story. He saw the deep heel marks of naked feet in parallel rows alongside the track and knew them to have been caused by the over-burdened carriers. He also saw places where they had put down their monstrous burden to rest.

He went very warily now, because he knew that cannon couldn't have been carried far under those conditions.

Suddenly, to his astonishment he found himself looking into the muzzle of that French-made gun.

It was planted in the middle of the trail, with its barrel facing back towards the settlement. At this point the trail was very narrow and straight, and brush wood had been piled round the gun so as to hide it.

Anyone riding along the trail would think that it wound round a brushy corner and wouldn't realize that the trail was obstructed until the very last moment.

Careless had his gun out, searching the bushes on every side of the cannon.

There was no movement. The gun had been deserted.

He rode closer and examined it with very great care. It was an elaborate piece of work, ornamented by craftsmen. There were eagles above the breach-block to act as sights and scorpions and snakes were chased along that barrel. It was the kind of gun that had once been made, but no longer did they put ornamentations on to artillery.

Careless didn't stay long. The gun examined to his satisfaction, he mounted again and rode rapidly back along the trail through the high trees towards the settlement. He didn't like leaving the girl alone.

He rode swiftly across the open ground in front of the settlement, and even as he rode he had a sudden premonition that all was not well within. He ducked through the tottering arch that had been the gateway into the settlement, and immediately his eyes were searching for the girl – and he couldn't see her or her horse!

In something almost a panic – an emotion unusual in that big man – Careless sent his horse thundering towards an alleyway that led down to the river. Then someone stood up within a ruined hut.

He saw a frantic face, and it was Jane's. She was beckoning to him, and by her gestures he knew she was begging him to be silent.

He swung his horse round and came riding swiftly across to that blackened shell. The girl was pointing between the buildings to where the river flowed swiftly by. She didn't say anything. She didn't need to.

Careless looked, and he was in time to see a horseman bring his mount at frantic pace out of the water. It was a Mexican wearing a sombrero.

His eyes switched, and he saw other horsemen frantically urging their beasts out of the river. He saw the man with woolly chaps whose name was Dave, and he saw those other three men whose identities were unknown to him.

And then he saw Major Abigay with them, and Sergeant Clay Holbein.

His eyes widened. His enemies had joined forces. Worse than that, they were coming right into the settlement.

At which exact moment Careless' eyes flitted across to the far bank and he saw the bobbing plumes of Indian horsemen as they came riding through the bushes towards the river—

Seven deadly enemies of the frontier agent came riding madly behind the shelter of those burnt-out huts.

Careless was still mounted. Jane had come running out of the burnt building and was clinging to his stirrup, her frightened eyes turned towards those riders.

There was a confused moment of hoofs digging into earth that was strewn with ashes, sending up choking clouds of dust. The horses were pulling back to an abrupt halt, sliding on their haunches – because those riders had seen the frontier agent and the girl before them.

Guns swung across and covered that mighty Texan. He didn't move. There was a mocking smile on his face as he looked at them, perspiring from their exertions and wet almost to the shoulders because of their frantic efforts to swim the river without being observed by those following Indians.

For a space of a few seconds all looked at each other. Then the Texan's drawling, ironic voice invited: 'Why don't you shoot?'

He felt the girl's hands grip his leg tightly at that. As if the thought of him being shot terrified her.

Still those guns covered him. Careless ignored them. He pushed Jane away and swung down, and never once did he attempt to go for his guns.

He said drily: 'You shoot me, pards, an' you bring the hull durned Comanche nation on top of you!'

He could still see through those buildings, and on the distant shore war-painted Indians were sitting their ponies, drinking gratefully from the water. It was evident that the two army men and the Border adventurers had entered this settlement without detection.

Careless started to lead his horse into that charred skeleton of a building where Jane's roan was meekly standing. Over his shoulder he jerked to those nonplussed enemies of his: 'I reckon for all our sakes you guys had better get yourselves hidden. Mebbe them Injuns won't bother to look inside the settlement when they cross the ford.'

He got inside that hut – a hut that was only

useful because part of two walls still remained and provided a screen from anyone crossing the river. He made himself comfortable. He even lit his pipe – that evil-smelling companion of the trail – knowing that from a distance the thin, wreathing smoke wouldn't be detected.

He saw those seven enemies of his confer together, and then they dismounted and led their horses inside another charred building.

When Careless next looked he saw that five men were keeping watch for the Indians – and two were keeping watch on them!

He saw two faces, and the protruding muzzles of two rifles which covered him from a distance of maybe thirty yards. Those two faces belonged to Major Abigay and the woolly chapped *hombre* known as Dave.

Between them they didn't intend him to get out of this settlement alive! Jane was shivering though the sun came through those blackened beams full upon them. She was afraid, but she wasn't afraid for herself – only for this big man who had befriended her and had been such a good trail companion.

She whispered: 'They're going to kill you, Careless!'

He puffed on his pipe. She saw him nod comfortably. He didn't seem at all bothered.

She laid her hand on his sleeve and there was impatience with her frantic concern. 'Careless, you don't seem to understand. They daren't shoot you now because of those Indians, and they're not going to let you get out of this place alive!'

She saw the big battered brown face that was so good-humoured turn to look at her, and she had a feeling that calmness flowed from him. It seemed to quieten the racing of her heart in an instant.

The Texan said quietly: 'I guess a lot of people have figgered to shorten my life.' He spread his hands and there was a grin on his face that made him look almost boyish. 'I'm still livin' – that shows how successful they've been!'

In spite of the situation – in spite of those two guns trained upon him – Jane found herself smiling, infected by his superb confidence.

She had a feeling that the resourceful frontier agent would not go out as easily as his enemies intended.

Then came a long period of tension for all those white people crouched within the settlement. They had seen the Indians grouped together on that far shore, and now the Comanches began to ford the river.

The sun glinted on sweaty brown bodies, and they caught the flash of light on silver horse-furniture.

Then the Comanches were riding through the shallows that led on to the west bank, and they were able to look on to those barbaric features, made hideous with war-paint that had become smudged and spread over their face and chests.

They could hear the harsh Comanche tongue being spoken, and they saw chiefs riding to whip up the stragglers. Those chiefs kept watching east-wards, as if expecting to see an enemy burst out upon the trail.

Then a procession quite two hundred strong began to ride round the edge of the charred palisade, no more than fifty yards from them. Now the white people were standing at the heads of their horses, pinching the velvety nostrils to prevent any betraying whinny from their beasts.

They saw that long column of Indians ride across the clearing towards the trail along which lay the Snata Anna cannon. The Indians rode in dejection like a proud people who have suffered defeat. This rearguard had evidently been soundly beaten in battle, for there were many wounded swaying in their saddles.

Suddenly Jane heard the big *hombre* say softly: 'Time we were leavin'!'

She turned in surprise. Those Indians were still streaming across the open space in front of the fortress – were still within sight of the charred ruin of a settlement.

Careless didn't say any more. He picked the girl up and placed her in her saddle and gave her the reins. Then he himself swung, with much creaking of leather protesting against his weight, into the saddle of his mighty horse.

It was at that moment that Major Abigay's voice crackled across to their ears – a subdued voice but one full of menace and passion.

'Where d'you think you're going, O'Connor? Get off them hosses, you two!'

Careless hitched himself into a more comfortable position, and then turned his perspiring face towards the major. The other Border adventurers had started to come out of that shell of a hut. They were walking menacingly towards the pair, guns in their hands, determination written on their faces – determined to prevent these two from escaping.

But they were still out of hands' reach. Careless just said politely: 'You go right ahead. Just fire those guns and see what good it does you!'

He said no more but deliberately rode out of the hut. The Border adventurers quickened their pace and broke into a run to try to catch up with them. They were putting their guns away because they knew they daren't fire and risk bringing those Indians back. Careless sent his horse into a trot. The Border gunnies were running fast now and he could look into straining, fiercely-angry faces.

He let Jane get ahead of him, and then followed her through the palisade gate.

The Indians at that moment disappeared into cover.

Jane realized that once outside the palisade big Careless had reined in his mount and was looking back at his enemies. Abigay and Dave came running up, so that all seven faced him, and yet they didn't attempt to leave that palisade – they knew it was useless, anyway.

They knew they had been outwitted by this big, clear-thinking, resourceful Texan. All the time he'd been one jump ahead of them!

It filled them with a fury so great that Abigay might have risked everything to down his enemy, but Sergeant Holbein dragged away the muzzle of his carbine and said something savagely under his breath to the officer.

They just stood there impotently, knowing that a step out of the palisade would result in the mounted pair galloping safely away. They still couldn't use their guns.

Careless spoke to them.

He looked at Major Abigay first, and he said: 'Mebbe I know now why Sergeant Holbein's able to blackmail you, major.'

The major's eyes were sharp with fury, but he said nothing. So Careless told him what he had found during his inspection of the cannon up the trail.

'You reported that you'd spiked that gun before allowing it to fall into enemy hands. The touch hole is free – it was never spiked. Major, as sure as I breathe, I'm goin' to get this report back to Army H.Q. I'm goin' to tell 'em that you sure don't deserve the rank they gave you!'

Abigay said nothing. There was nothing for him to say.

Then Careless looked at the sergeant and he spoke softly: 'Sergeant Holbein, there was an artilleryman who got away with you from Rattlesnake. He died durin' some fightin' at Whitesides.'

Sergeant Holbein lifted his head inquiringly. His face was red from exertion and dirty where his dusty sleeve had been used to wipe away the sweat.

Careless went on, still in that soft voice: 'You should know how that artilleryman died, sergeant. You should know why he died, an' then mebbe you'll understand why Major Abigay was so insistent that you come out with him on this trip.'

The sergeant had turned quickly, and was looking Abigay full in the eye. He wasn't understanding yet, but he was a mighty suspicious man. Abigay licked his lips, his fury again almost beyond control. He growled: 'It's a lie, whatever he says, Holbein! Don't you believe him!'

Careless was manoeuvring his mount so as to keep it between the sun and those tense figures standing just within the palisade gateway.

He said abruptly, contemptuously: 'What's a lie? I haven't said anything yet.'

Holbein, that mottle-faced, blue-chinned sergeant, was looking at his superior officer – was seeing the black wrath in that lean, weathered face. He asked quickly: 'What are you talkin' about? What's this about Hardy?'

Deliberately Careless leaned forward from his saddle, his eyes hard and merciless as they watched that promotion-hungry officer. For a second he thought that the man was going to use his gun to silence him. And then the gun-muzzle depressed. Careless still had them in his palm, because none of them dared risk bringing those Indians back upon them.

Careless said harshly: 'That man Hardy knew that Abigay had run away without spiking that gun. He was a good soldier, an' he knew it was wrong to let a gun like that fall into enemy hands. He kept threatening to tell the army H.Q. about the incident, and Abigay must have decided to silence him.'

Abigay, crouching there in the sunshine, the picture of black fury, called hoarsely: 'I keep tellin' you, Holbein. This fellar's got a lyin' tongue.'

But Holbein was listening only to Careless. He growled: 'You go on.'

'He took his chance durin' a surprise Injun attack at Whitesides. That soldier went runnin' to fight the Injuns. Abigay shot him from behind. He thought no one knew anythin' about that crime, but Jane Frazer here,' – his hand indicated the girl – 'put two an' two together.'

Holbein's head was turning to look at his superior officer. He was a hard, brutal man, himself. He wasn't above blackmail, and it hadn't seemed such a serious matter to run away and leave that gun to an enemy.

But he'd never committed murder. He could never have killed a man who had slept and fought at his side like that good young chap called Hardy.

Careless pressed home the point. He was doing all this deliberately. Careless O'Connor never did a thing without reason.

Right now he wanted to split the enemy, and so make them less effective. His voice was softer now, and yet to that major it was just as hosile.

'Y'know what I think. Holbein?' Holbein's face came away from Abigay and looked into Careless' brown, sweating It seemed that Holbein was already guessing, but he waited to hear what O'Connor had to say.

'I reckon Abigay brought you into Injun territory with the idea of silencin' you the same way. You were getting awkward and dangerous, with your drinkin' and blackmailin'. Yeah, I figger he wanted you out of the way like Hardy.'

Holbein just growled: 'I reckon I owe you my

thanks, O'Connor. I hadn't thought Abigay was such a louse.' He said that deliberately, facing his superior officer, and so enraged now at the other man's treachery that his words were a challenge to action.

But Abigay valued life more than anything. And gunplay now would have brought the Indians back and terminated his life for certain. He just stood there, glaring hatred, but taking the insults.

Holbein said: 'I'll be watchin' him from now on, O'Connor. He won't do me any harm. I'll get him first if he tries.'

Suddenly Abigay turned and walked back into the settlement. They watched him approach his horse, and they knew what that meant. Abigay was going to ride alone in the wilderness. They didn't know where he was going or what was in his mind, but clearly he had decided to break away from that party. With Holbein in it there was no future for him.

O'Connor watched that lean artillery officer stalk in among the debris, his boots kicking up a dust that was nearly white because of the wood ash contained within it. He said softly: 'Sergeant, I figger that guy's goin' to try to shut your mouth. Watch out for him!'

Holbein nodded.

Careless looked at those other five despera-does. There was humour in his eyes, though contempt lingered there with it. Very softly he asked, 'How's Reiffel?'

Those five men just stood like statues, their faces as impassive as any marble sculpting. Not by a flicker of an eyelid did they betray anything.

Careless started to pull his horse round and it did some kicking, anxious to get out of this blazing sunshine and into the coolness of those trees across the glade. Careless nodded. 'OK,' he drawled. 'You don't need to tell me. But I know who sent you here, an' I know somethin' you don't know!'

They looked interested.

He said softly: 'I know what you think you're after, but you're wrong, brothers, dead wrong. Reiffel's usin' you like he's used others before you. You won't come out of this as well as you think.'

And again he was deliberately sowing the seeds of suspicion. He was making guesses, but he was pretty sure he was right.

He'd said enough. If he stayed much longer, the Indians would be out of sound of gun fire, and then he would be at their mercy.

He saw the lean Major Abigay ride out of the settlement through a gap in the north palisade. He was heading up river. Careless nodded to the men and sent his horse galloping across the glade to where the foothills rose to the west of the settlement. Jane came riding beside him. They went in among the cool shady trees and then Careless dropped to a walking pace and proceeded with great caution.

Jane smiled at him. Her eyes were admiring. She said: 'I've never met a man like you. It doesn't matter how desperate the situation, you never seem to get flurried, and you always seem to pull something out of the bag.'

He grinned at her from his bigger horse, and he drawled: 'You keep talkin' an' I'll have to pull somethin' else out of the bag.' His eyes swept round the pleasant greenery. 'These parts must be alive with Comanches now,' he said softly. 'Better not talk. Voices carry a long way.'

They began to climb through the woods, and after a time the way became very steep and the trees thinned until in time they were walking on the bare hillside. That worried Careless until he found a rain gully, which gave them pretty good cover all the way up the mountainside.

Jane knew she could talk now, because there could be no lurking enemies near to them.

She asked: 'Where are we going, Careless?'

He said: 'Not far. I want to get higher so that we can look down upon things.'

He shoved back that sweat-stained hat and turned in his saddle to look back the way they had come. He was looking over the green trees that seemed to choke the valley below. It was so well wooded that the trail that he knew wound through it remained unseen even from that height.

He said: 'Them Injuns have got that gun into position across the trail. I figger they put it there in case they got licked an' had to retreat into the hills.'

That narrow gorge, through which the trail ran up to the gun, would be a perfect death trap. Troops massed along the trail at that point would be mown down by shot from that powerful cannon.

Careless was thinking what he would do if he was an Indian chief. He would have men hidden along the wooded heights that overlooked that trail. He would open fire with that hidden cannon when the advancing American forces were almost riding on to the gun muzzle. There would be a scene of carnage, as round after round of heavy iron shot screeched through the packed troops along that narrow, straight trail, and then the waiting Indians on the heights at either side would rise and pour a deadly hail of arrows upon the trapped soldiers beneath.

Careless could see it all in his mind's eye. Now he wanted to get into a position where he could overlook this territory and see if the Indians were planning just as he imagined.

They walked now, leading their lathered horses up that rocky gully. Then they came out upon a part of the hillside that had been swept away in a landslide. Careless halted and looked at the raw rock face for a while until he saw something that satisfied him.

He turned to Jane and said: 'We're there.' His head jerked towards a black cleft among the rocks. 'That looks mighty like a cave big enough to hide us an' our hosses.'

He led the way out of the gully, and now they ran the risk of detection as they scrambled across the bare rock face that must have looked so prominent from below. But they had to take risks.

Within a few minutes they were at the entrance of that natural cave. Careless told her to wait outside and hold the horses, while he went in cautiously, his Sharps at the ready.

He went inside sniffing the air, and halting every few paces to let his eyes adjust to the light.

The girl heard him call to her: 'OK, Jane, you can come in.' When she came inside he said: 'I figgered there might be a bear livin' here. But there ain't.'

It was a relief to go into that cool dark cavern after the blinding hot sunshine outside. But Careless' thought was for the horses which had so gallantly borne them along the hard trail. He poured water down their eager, gasping throats, and then unsaddled them and rubbed them down.

Then, but only then, he drank himself and ate some of the dried meat that was in his pack. Jane

107

felt too exhausted to eat, but was grateful for the lukewarm water.

The big Texan seemed tireless, however. He didn't even sit down to rest while he ate. All the time his eyes were watching the opening that revealed the bright blue Arizona sky. He was a man always alert, always suspecting danger. While he was still chewing a last hunk of meat, he began to walk towards the entrance of that cavern.

Jane at once sat up and asked: 'Where are you going?'

Careless' answer filled her with dread: 'Guess I'm just goin' out a while. I figger I ought to keep a watch on the trail, an' I can't do that here.'

Jane ran across to him. He saw the fear on her lovely face. She put her arms about him as if she would restrain him physically.

She exclaimed: 'Oh, Careless, don't leave me here!'

Careless smiled and stroked the soft brown hair. 'You're safer here than up on the mountainside. Nope, Jane, I figger you've got to stay with the hosses.'

Gently he disengaged her hands and turned and walked out of the cave, leaving her to stare fearfully after him.

Jane had more than a normal amount of courage, but after the last day's incidents she felt very weak and small without the protection of that big, drawling Texan.

Careless climbed quickly but carefully on to a shoulder of the bare mountainside that lifted out on to a gigantic bluff. He guessed that once on the edge of that bluff, and he would have a magnificent view for miles around. It took him half an hour to gain the bluff, but then he wormed his way on his stomach to the crumbling edge of the mighty cliff and looked down.

It was like a picture from a child's book. He looked down upon the land as if it were a map. Now he could see that trail from the ford quite clearly. And he could see the winding Rattlesnake River for miles up and down its green edged course.

His eyes turned westward over a low range of hills that gave out on to another great plain that ended where a mighty mountain range reared snow-white peaks into the glorious blue sky.

Then his eyes narrowed. He found himself looking upon a whole town of tipis. The Comanches were encamped in all their might just beyond that wooded ridge below.

He watched them for minutes on end. He saw the great circles of tents, and he saw people all the time moving between them, and he knew that thousands were encamped there. He knew, too, that the women and children had moved into this camp, and that made the situation even more ominous.

It meant that the Comanches would fight the

more bitterly with their weaker ones so close upon their heels.

He watched and saw that in fact the camp was being taken down, and some people with burdened horses were already beginning the westwards trek. But at the rate work was going on, it was evident that the main tribe could not be moved back into the safety of those mighty mountains within the next few hours.

That thought brought his eyes swinging to the wooded country east of the Rattlesnake River. He thought, 'They're not goin' to get more than a few hours' start, anyway.'

For he saw, like fantastically small toys, the figures of several men with their horses drinking on the eastern bank of the Rattler. He knew them to be scouts of the American army.

He looked beyond, into the green trees that clothed the distant plain, and he began to detect movement among them, and then realized that the whole of the American force was riding towards the ford at the Rattlesnake settlement.

Now again his eyes swung down to the trail, looking for that high-walled, straight section threatened by the cannon that had been Santa Anna's favourite.

He rose upon his hands, his eyes intent, caught by a movement below.

The Border adventurers had found the gun.

SEVEN

DEATH OF A HERO!

He saw those six riders on the trail where an obstruction showed where the cannon lay. He saw one of the riders detach himself and ride westwards over the ridge. He wore a blue tunic, so he knew that it would be Sergeant Holbein, Careless thought, 'He's wary. He's goin' to make sure no Injuns come ridin' back along that trail.'

The other men were dismounting and examining the gun under its brushwood camouflage.

The Texan's eyes flickered towards the Indian camp. He started. A small group of Indians was riding out of the camp towards the trail over the ridge.

Careless thought, 'They're gonna run slap bang into that sergeant.' It wasn't pleasant to have to watch that scene and not be able to warn the distant artillery sergeant. All he could do was lie up there and see the lone horseman ride steadily towards that advancing group of braves.

The sergeant must have gained the ridge ahead of those Indians. Careless saw the lone, blue-shirted horseman halt abruptly. Then he saw Holbein swing his horse round and go galloping like mad towards the other five men grouped around that cannon.

He must have seen the approaching Indians, and he'd turned immediately to escape from them and warn his companions.

But looking down upon the scene Careless realized that those Indians hadn't seen the artillery sergeant. Their pace hadn't changed. They were still riding their tired ponies up towards the crest of the hill. Probably by the time they reached it Sergeant Holbein had turned a bend in the trail and was out of sight.

Careless watched the little drama. He saw Holbein race madly towards the camouflaged gun – saw the scattering of those five other men as they dived for their horses. Then the whole party disappeared among the trees.

Careless watched for about half an hour longer. In that time he didn't see the six white men again. Either they had gone to ground or they were still riding steadily away from this dangerous area.

He kept watching that eastern bank. The scouts had forded the river, but hadn't moved away from the charred rectangle that had been a thriving community only a few weeks back. Careless saw the militia come into view on the east bank, followed by the lumbering artillery. They didn't attempt the crossing immediately, evidently deciding upon rest before invading the hostile west bank.

During this time that group of Indians had gained the hidden cannon on the trail. A few of them continued to ride on to the edge of the forest, and most of the way Careless was able to look down upon them and see them in gaps through the trees. After a while one of the Indians came spurring back, passing his companions at the gun without pause.

Careless thought: 'He's gone to tell his tribe that the white men are hard on their heels.'

He had a feeling that the Indians had been surprised by the swiftness of the white men's advance. With the arrival of the scout into the Indian camp, the activity became feverish.

Tipis were brought down, and a continuous procession strung out across the flat land leading towards the mountains. But the braves didn't go with them. Careless saw them leap for their horses and come charging along the trail. Hundreds of braves jammed that trail right up to the point where the cannon was situated.

And then Careless saw the Indians do just as he had guessed they would. The main body of Indians camped back with the horses in the depths of the wood behind the gun. But two other parties dismounted and went climbing to the heights immediately above where the trail ran through that gorge.

Within minutes the ambush was completed. Careless looked, but could only see the waiting main body of Indian cavalry resting among the trees to the rear of the cannon. The braves on top of the cliffs were completely hidden from sight.

He looked eastward, and saw the first of the militia begin to cross the river. At that he began to climb down the hillside towards the cave. He had seen enough. Now was the time for action.

Before, his object had been that cannon. Now a matter of greater importance had risen.

At all costs he must prevent those soldiers from riding into a death trap.

Jane cried out gladly when he came swinging into the cavern from the rocky ledge that ran above the entrance. She ran into his arms and held him as if she would never let him go. She'd been a very scared girl alone in that cavern.

'I kept thinking a bear might come while you were away,' she said. Her eyes were brimming with tears of joy and relief at seeing him.

He hated to have to say it, but he had to tell her: 'Sorry, Jane, but I've got to leave you again. The Injuns have got a trap sprung, an' the militia are sure headin' for their death.'

When he said that Jane let him go. She wasn't

going to keep him away from his duty.

Again he left her with his horse. What he had to do didn't require a horse. He went slithering down the mountainside until he came to the tree line, and then the way grew more level and easier, but he ran recklessly, because he didn't have much time.

But when he reached the bottomland, where the brushwood was thicker under the trees, caution returned to his movements. He knew that the Indians wore grouped at three points along that trail, and he didn't think he was likely to run across a stray party of Comanche braves, but he couldn't afford to take risks.

He was undecided yet on his plan. He knew he couldn't get round the Indians in time to warn the U.S. soldiers before they walked into this valley of death. Back of his mind was the idea of lying up alongside that trail, so that as the first American cavalry came in sight he could warn them with a sudden shot.

He didn't think what would happen to himself afterwards. All he thought about then was warning his people before they walked on to that deadly cannon mouth.

He was crawling now, proceeding with even greater caution as he came nearer the trail. He passed through thick blackjack thorns, and they plucked at his shirt and tore it, and then he had to cross some open ground before he came to some more thorns.

He went swiftly across that little glade, and no shout of warning came up from an Indian throat. He went quietly, cautiously in among those dark thorns, worming his way forward until suddenly he realized that the trail was right ahead of him.

Suddenly he was so close to that trail that he could see the Indians grouped around the gun. They were silent. He saw their impassive, bronzed features, and saw that their eyes were intent on one thing only – the end of the trail where it ran through the high-walled gorge.

He was just moving cautiously to get a view of that gun and see if it were loaded, when something crashed upon his head. He saw lights that swiftly faded as unconsciousness gripped him. The strength went out of his mighty arms and legs, and he slumped on his face in the dirt.

Seconds later he began to recover. His eyes opened dazedly, and he thought that the earth was slipping away from under him. To his spinning senses it seemed that everywhere there was movement – that even trees and bushes slowly moved.

Then a pressure on his neck made him realize that someone was furtively, slowly dragging him deeper into those bushes. He hadn't the strength to resist.

Suddenly, where sunshine found a way through the thick growth overhead, the pressure on his neck was released. He turned his head. Men were sitting behind him, their faces sweating from exertion and from fear of what might happen if their actions betrayed them to the crouching Indians on the trail.

His eyes saw the Mexican's brown ones first. Then Dave and the other gunmen came into focus. Last of all, Sergeant Holbein stood before him.

They had their guns out again, covering him, yet they were useless to them now as they had been before. But this time Careless knew that he was very much their prisoner. They would not need to use their guns and thus betray themselves; if necessary they could use force in other ways, more silently.

He didn't feel like using force himself at that moment. The strength was rapidly returning to him, but that blow on the head had been a cruel one and had sapped him of his normal vitality. He was content for the moment to lie there and recover and look at those men.

Dave, his thin face vicious, whispered: 'What d'you know about that cannon?'

Careless didn't answer him.

Dave grabbed him by the shirt front, and now he hissed, 'You were right, O'Connor, that gun didn't have what we thought it had. Reiffel let us think some wrong things, I guess.'

Careless sat up and suddenly knocked that hand away from his shirt. He never did tolerate any man laying hands on him. But Dave crouched there before him, squatting menacingly on his heels, that six-shooter raised aloft in a threat to his aching head again.

Careless said sardonically: 'I guess you guys thought there'd be sheets of gold wrapped round the barrel. Or mebbe all them ornaments on that gun would turn out to be pure silver underneath the paintwork.' His eyes swept round contemptuously at the six men – for it seemed that Holbein had thrown in his lot with the gunmen.

'You don't think Reiffel would've picked men like you to retrieve a gun that was covered with solid lumps of gold or silver, do you?'

Those men shifted uneasily before his withering sarcasm. Because it was evident that they had thought that gun would contain precious metal.

Careless rubbed his head tenderly. 'You guys took Reiffel's money when he grubstaked you on this expedition. But I figger all the time back of your minds was the thought of doin' a double-cross on him – huh?' His statement ended with a quick sound of interrogation.

Dave was looking more malevolent than ever, and Careless didn't have to hear an admission of guilt. One look at Dave's face and he knew that he'd guessed right.

He could laugh at them, knowing how stupid they had been. Reiffel had let them believe that he wanted that gun because of something precious it contained – and these gunmen would think naturally in terms of precious metal, like gold. And naturally they would plan to get that gun and keep the gold for themselves. Reiffel could whistle for his money after that.

'It just hasn't turned out as you planned,' Careless said softly, mockingly.

One of the gunmen growled savagely. 'It don't look to have turned out right for you, either, Mr Frontier Agent.'

But Dave interrupted him with an impatient gesture. 'Shut your face,' he snarled. 'That gun don't contain what we thought it did – gold. But there's somethin' mighty valuable about it, or Reiffel would never have paid us five hundred dollars on account and promised us ten thousand more if we got that gun safely back to him.'

He licked his lips, hatred in those snapping brown eyes of his. He had personal reasons for disliking the big Texan, quite apart from the fact that Careless had a knowledge greater than his own.

He said unpleasantly, 'You know what's valuable about that gun. You're gonna tell us!'

Lying helplessly in their midst in that thorn grove, Careless could yet jeer back at them. 'What good will it do you if you do know? It's nothin' you'd understand.'

Sergeant Holbein came into the conversation then, his voice low and growling.

'I don't understand things at all.' His eyes flickered meanly towards Dave, the ringleader of these gunmen. 'I quit the army an hour back, when they promised me a cut in whatever they got out of that cannon.'

'They told you it was solid gold?' asked Careless ironically.

'They did, an' I was fool enough to believe it. But we dug our knives into that gun, and there ain't no gold that I can see about it. Now I want to know who's this man Reiffel everybody's talkin' about?'

They all looked at Careless. Dave said menacingly, 'Mebbe Mister Smarty knows more about Reiffel than we do, too.'

Careless nodded, his eyes bleak and his face grim. 'I guess I do,' he rapped. Then he added, 'But I don't open my mouth about Reiffel any more than I do about that gun. The only thing I can say to you guys is – you'll never get this gun out of these hills, an' if you did you wouldn't be doin' yourselves any good!'

The men looked uneasily at each other then. One of them, a big, surly brute who hadn't shaved for a week, said unpleasantly, 'He ain't tellin' us anythin' we don't know.' His hand gestured through the bushes towards the trail where the Indians were lurking. 'We can't get that gun away with them Injuns sittin' around it.'

Careless said softly, 'Those few Injuns that are on the gun ain't nothin' to worry about. Half the

Comanche army's camped in the woods back of the trail. The other's half's split in two, watching down the gorge from the cliff tops.'

They hadn't realized that. They stared at the big Texan. He went on speaking without waiting for them to ask questions. He was sitting up now and his face was hard and purposeful. He knew he had to work quickly, because time was slipping by.

Now it had become a race, in fact. The American soldiers must be very near to the beginning of that gorge – that death-trap in the hills. He had to get away from these men in time to warn them, or else he had to persuade them to give that warning themselves.

But as he looked around at their hard-bitten features, his heart sank. These were the kind of men who thought only of themselves. They weren't likely to endanger their own lives in an effort to save the lives of those advancing soldiers.

But he could try. He said, 'There's an army of militia ridin' along the trail towards us right now. They're shovin' the Comanches back where they came from, an' they'll be along this trail any time in the next half-hour, I reckon.'

His hand waved towards where they knew those Indians were crouching around that captured cannon.

'Them Comanches have fixed a deathtrap for those soldiers. I reckon some of 'em have been around army forts an' know how to fire a gun. I guess it's loaded now, an' when that narrow gorge is full of American soldiers, that cannon'll blast 'em off the face of the earth. They've got to be warned! They can't be allowed to ride to their deaths in that manner!'

Dave said harshly, 'I don't care about the army. All I want to know is – what is the secret of that gun?'

Careless' eyes were blazing. He said: 'You'll never find out from me. You ought to be hung for what you've just said. Now let me go and I'll warn the troops before they get into this ambush.'

One of the men came up and whispered something in Dave's ear. Dave looked sourly at the Texan and then nodded slowly.

He said, 'We don't know how much of what you've told us is the truth. Mebbe there ain't no trap. Mebbe there ain't no American army. So I guess we just get away into the hills until these Injuns clear off, then we'll come back and get that gun.' But that sergeant was suddenly pushing his way in front of the leader of the gunmen.

He was an ugly brute, that man, with his blotchy, raw-red face and scrub beard on his fleshy jowl. He had mean eyes and a meaner character.

But just as he had revolted at the thought of a comrade being shot down by his own officer, so now Sergeant Clay Holbein revolted at the idea of letting his comrades walk to their death.

He growled, 'I ain't gonna stand by an' see

them galoots ride to their death!'

The other rannies looked at him, startled. Dave growled, 'What're you gonna do, soldier?'

The sergeant shook his head doggedly. He was in the same fix as Careless a few minutes ago. 'I don't know what I can do; all I know is I'm gonna do somethin'. Mebbe when I see 'em comin' round the trail, I'll just fire my gun in the air an' alert 'em.'

Dave looked at him with eyes that just didn't understand. He said, 'You'll die for that.'

The sergeant said, 'OK, I'll die. Better me die than hundreds of my kind.'

He had made up his mind. He was a soldier, and, unlike these renegades, he was loyal to his kind. Careless looked at the sergeant and said, 'Man – you're a man! I'm proud to know you, you old son-of-a-gun!'

Dave's gun was covering that sergeant. He said, 'I don't care what you do. It ain't my life you're riskin'. But one thing I know. I'm not gonna leave this big *hombre* walkin' around on his two legs. He's kinda got a habit of upsettin' me.'

Careless grinned at him. He said, 'If you're thinkin' of endin' my life, just think, brother. If I die, you'll never know the value of that gun out there.'

His eyes had caught a movement in the bushes behind those rannies. He was sure it wasn't the movement of an Indian, either, because he had caught the merest hint of cloth – and the

Comanches on the warpath didn't wear clothes other than a breech-clout.

He switched his eyes away, not wishing to give warning to these rannies. He couldn't conceive who might be lurking back there, but in the tight corner that he found himself now it could hardly make matters worse for him, whoever it was.

Therein Careless made a mistake – a great mistake.

Dave was taking some cord from out of his pocket. 'I got all that figgered out,' he rasped. 'I'm gonna tie you up an' leave you here, hid up under a bush. I ain't gonna stay around these parts if a battle's gonna start. But I aim to come back when it's all over and collect that gun.

'I aim to collect you, too, if you've lived through it, an' I reckon when I've got more time I'll sure dig the truth out of you!'

His eyes were vicious. It was tantalizing to feel that that gun contained something of vast worth, and yet he couldn't detect the secret. But Dave wasn't the kind of man to give in easily. He was determined to discover that secret somehow.

He tied Careless' hands behind him and rolled him out of sight where the thorns grew thickest. He was out of sight but he could see.

He saw those rannies look at the sergeant, and he saw the sergeant look at them as if he hated them suddenly.

Dave growled, 'You're on your own now,

soldier. We're quittin', I reckon.'

The sergeant growled back. 'I'm quittin', too. I'm goin' as far along that trail as I can crawl, an' then I'm gonna hole up until I see that flag I've served all these years. Then—'

He didn't finish his sentence. He had stated his intentions before, and it was clear that he was unwavering in his determination.

Careless watched them as they turned to push their way out through those bushes, no doubt to find their horses, hidden away from the trail.

He saw Dave lead the way and the other four men follow, and then the squat sergeant started to go after them. The sergeant didn't so much as look at Careless. It was a matter of indifference to him what happened to the big Texan now.

Careless suddenly saw a movement behind that sergeant. Someone was lifting out of the bushes, rearing behind the blue-shirted artilleryman.

Careless saw the flash of a knife, and then Sergeant Clay Holbein, a man with every intention of being a hero, collapsed like a punctured balloon in the scrub.

Those five gunmen walked on without knowing what had happened behind their backs.

Holbein's killer turned and walked deliberately to where Careless was lying bound helpless in those bushes.

It was Major Morris Abigay.

EIGHT

MEDICINE MAN

Lying there, Careless' first thought was not of danger to himself. When he saw Holbein collapse, his thoughts were: 'The troops won't be warned now! There's no one to let them know they're walking into a death trap!' It brought him sitting up, though the thorns from the low, spreading bushes scratched his head. He wrestled furiously with those cords, but they had been tightly, expertly fixed around his wrists. His eyes were furious as they looked at that advancing officer, the triumph blazing in those eyes, that knife red with the life-blood of the unfortunate sergeant.

Careless rolled out from under that bush. They were together now, in a tiny open space, in the middle of those dense thorns. They were separated by no more than three or four yards.

Abigay halted as he saw the giant Texan rear up on his feet. But reassurance came to him immediately as he realized that Careless' hands were securely tied behind him.

Abigay snarled. 'You've caused me enough trouble. You ain't gonna live, O'Connor. You an' Holbein knew too much. Holbein's gone and now you're goin', too.'

Careless exclaimed: 'Man, can't you forget yourself for a minute? The army's walkin' into a death trap. Go and give them warning, for heaven's sake!'

Abigay didn't even seem to hear him. He was moving slowly nearer, that knife poised ready to strike. Looking at him, Careless knew that this officer had no thought beyond his own safety. He wasn't fit to wear the uniform that was on his back at that moment.

Careless knew that, for all Abigay cared, the whole United States army could walk to its doom. The thought filled the bound man with a raging fury that he had never known before.

Careless leapt forward, just at the moment when Abigay came leaping in, that knife upraised, to strike him down.

Careless' quick movement saved him. He was actually inside the blow as it descended, and his shoulder crashed into Abigay's chest and sent the man hurtling painfully into the thorn scrub.

Abigay was on his feet in a flash, that knife

127

gripped even tighter for a death-blow.

It was a fantastic fight – a fight between a killer armed with a long knife and a man bound and seemingly helpless.

To make it even more fantastic, they had to fight in silence, because no more than thirty or forty yards away, savage Comanche Indians crouched around the cannon on that trail. Noise would bring those Indians upon them, and then neither would live.

Abigay dived recklessly forward at O'Connor, mouthing curses under his breath as he did so. He was going to finish off this big Texan without any further waste of time, he was snarling.

Careless threw himself headfirst at Abigay's feet. The major, not expecting this move, tripped over that solid Texan's body and came down on his face.

Careless rolled at once, throwing his weight along the prostrate Abigay's back. The Texan's eyes were seeking for that knife hand. He was trying to roll with his back on top of that knife, desperately seeking to grasp it with his bound hands and tear it away from the major.

Abigay was too quick for him. The major reared, and Careless was thrown onto his back. Abigay came whirling round in a fury of activity, trying to knife Careless before he could rise to his feet.

Frantically Careless rolled and got out of range

and then came to his feet. Abigay was still plunging across, and Careless kicked and his boot
smacked into the wrist of the hand that held the
knife. The knife flew away and fell behind Abigay.
Abigay grasped his pained wrist, but had the
sense to go wheeling round and dive instantly to
recover his knife.

Then they were right back where they started.
Abigay circled with that gleaming knife in his
hand, his face a picture of almost insane ferocity.
And Careless, his hands tied behind him, all the
while kept away from the direction of Abigay's
movement.

Careless watched those sharp pinpoints of fury
that were Abigay's eyes, knowing they would tell
him when attack was contemplated.

Suddenly he saw them widen slightly, and he
knew – 'This is it!'

Abigay came lurching across, and again he
began to snarl and his hand rose to deliver a
deadly blow. But this time Careless went in to
finish his opponent.

As the major came leaping across Careless
threw himself into a sideways roll. He thrust one
leg stiffly before him, while the other leg crooked
and came round behind the major's knees.

Abigay found his shins striking against that
stiffly extended leg; before he could recover,
Careless' worn boot cracked him in the bend of
his knees and he found himself neatly tripped.

Abigay had been moving at speed, and was off his balance. Before he could recover himself he went headlong to the ground again.

This time he didn't try to get to his feet.

Careless had come leaping up, ready to use his feet – the only weapons he had. But he saw there was no need for it. Abigay was out. His head had crashed against a blackthorn tree stump that was as hard as twisted steel.

Panting the victor of that unequal combat swayed across to where Abigay still clutched that knife in his hand. Careless dropped to the ground, his eyes watching the major for a sign of a return to consciousness. Behind his back his hands sought for that knife – found it and dragged it away from the clutch of those hooked fingers.

He swayed to his feet again, and tried desperately with his bound hands to get the knife-blade working against the cord that fastened his wrists together. He felt that he wasn't making much progress. Then Abigay groaned and stirred.

Now it was a race between that knife and Abigay's return to consciousness.

Frantically Careless sawed at those bonds. Abigay stirred and his head came round. Careless looked into eyes that were glazed. He began to retreat among those thorns, heading away from where those Indians were lurking on the trail. And all the time he sawed away with that knife.

Abigay began to pull himself erect. Those bonds seemed as impregnable as ever. Careless kept rubbing the knife blade as well as he could against the cords, and he began to run across the open glade towards that other, denser thorn scrub. He heard Abigay come to his feet and begin to stagger after him.

Now it was a game – but a deadly game – of hide and seek. Careless had to keep moving, had to keep dodging from cover to cover in order to give himself time to break through those bonds. He could feel now that some strands had been severed. Perhaps in a few moments he would be free and then he could face up to Abigay on more equal terms.

Abigay hunted him relentlessly. Now he seemed indifferent to the possibility of being discovered by the Comanches.

He was probably half-crazed by that crack on his head. Naturally vengeful, Abigay couldn't tolerate this succession of defeats at the hands of the big Texan. To be licked by an unarmed man whose hands were bound behind him was some-thing that seemed to turn Abigay's mind to madness.

Recklessly Abigay plunged through those thorn bushes, seeking for glimpses of his quarry, and all the time following as fast as he could.

He got O'Connor cornered. The thorn scrub gave out at this point and there was only a great open space beyond. Careless couldn't go running across it, because he felt sure that Indians on the height above the trail would see him. He had to turn at bay and face his other enemy.

Abigay had his revolver out. He was holding it by the barrel, intending to use it as a club.

The knife dropped from Careless' hands.

Careless felt a great surge of anger sweep over him at that fresh disaster. Everything seemed to be against him. Just a few minutes more and he could have got through those bonds, he thought.

Abigay leapt towards him, and this time he was going to finish off his big adversary.

The fury that gripped Careless seemed to swell the muscles of his mighty arms. He exerted all his strength, and suddenly the half-severed cords snapped.

Abigay, aghast, within reach of his enemy, suddenly saw those mighty fists come from behind O'Connor, the frayed cord trailing from the wrists.

Abigay never knew what hit him. O'Connor smacked home one blow only. It caught Abigay in mid-air, in the final moment of his leap. The fist crashed against the unprotected jaw and Abigay went down as if he would never rise again.

Panting, Careless stooped over him, and picked up the revolver that had fallen from the major's hand. That was his only weapon now.

He didn't stay with Abigay. Abigay didn't count

now. Instead he looked through the trees and tried to see the sun – tried to estimate what time had elapsed since he'd been ambushed by the side of the trail.

He knew that time was running out. If the U.S. soldiers weren't already in that pass, then they must be very near to it. Careless went plunging back through the thorn bushes.

He saw the sergeant lying on his face. He didn't pause as he passed because he knew that the man was dead.

He ran on, recklessly now, that gun in his hand. He found himself suddenly running out on to the trail, round a bend from where the gun had been placed.

And he found himself looking at the weirdest apparition he had ever seen. He saw a human skull. It was worn in the middle of a body that was decorated with human bones. He saw a death mask that was in bright colours, surmounted by great curving buffalo horns. He saw racoons' tails, and feathers from many birds.

It was a scarecrow of an individual. He had run into the Comanche Medicine Man.

NINE

WHERE IS JANE?

Careless had an impression that the trail at this point was deserted save for their two selves. He had an instinct that the Medicine Man was going forward, perhaps to hearten the men around that gun with his fierce war talk.

And he had an impression of a very scared Medicine Man who thought only of turning and fleeing before this mighty white man who had come bounding out of the bushes.

Twenty seconds later that Medicine Man was sleeping as soundly as Abigay back among the thorn bushes. Half a minute later and he was naked and tied so that he would not move again in a hurry.

And out on the trail that big Texan was getting into the death mask, and was pulling on that hideous garment of bones and feathers and furry tails. Careless O'Connor had decided to be a Medicine Man!

He started to walk quickly up the trail towards the gun. Now his intention was to walk boldly past those Indian gunners, and keep on walking down that trail until he met the advancing American troops. The move would cause consternation, but no Indian would open fire against a Medicine Man.

To Careless it seemed as though luck had turned his way at last, meeting that Medicine Man.

He rounded the bend in the trail, and there before him he saw those Indians crouching to the rear of that camouflaged cannon. They looked at him in awe as he approached, but no one spoke. Then from the heights alongside that long, straight trail, they heard the sharp cough of a mountain lion.

Instantly the Medicine Man was forgotten. Those Indians whirled to look down the trail. Careless realized what that signal meant. Within sight of those watchers on the cliffs were the advancing American troops. They must be about to enter the deathtrap.

There was no time now for advancing down that trail. O'Connor deliberately pulled out his revolver and pressed the trigger. He was committing suicide by doing so, he knew, but it was the only way he could alert the white men before they walked into this trap.

Nothing happened. He pressed the trigger again. There was a click as the firing pin failed to meet the cartridge cap.

Horrified, O'Connor looked at the revolver in his hand. He realized that it was empty. He hadn't thought to check up on it when he tore it away from Abigay's nerveless grip.

His own ammunition wouldn't fit this Service revolver. It was useless to him. He lifted his head in despair and saw that it was too late now to warn those troops.

Already they had begun to march down that valley of death.

Careless looked round desperately. Then he saw a bow and a sheath of arrows lying to the side of the trail, probably put there by one of the men at the cannon. He ran back and picked them up. He took an arrow and strung it and then turned towards the gun again.

An Indian had some smouldering cloth in a little pot. Now he took a piece and advanced towards the touch-hole of that cannon. Once that glowing cloth fell in among the powder, the charge would explode and the cannon ball go screaming into those packed American ranks riding in at the end of the valley.

But that Indian didn't explode the charge immediately. He held the light above the touch-hole, obviously waiting until the last moment, when the valley would be packed with American soldiers and the leaders be almost on to the cannon mouth.

Careless did some quick thinking. He stood there, that arrow strung to his bow, while over the top of the brushwood he watched the advance of the cavalry. He knew that on either side of that pass Indians would be waiting for the signal for the attack to begin.

He guessed now that that signal would be the exploding of the cannon.

He had decided that that cannon wouldn't fire – that the signal would never be given.

He turned his head. Lurking in the depths of the wood along the trail from him would be the main army of the Comanches, waiting for that same signal for them to emerge and charge upon a stricken force. But for the moment there were no Indians in sight behind him.

The cavalry were filling that valley now, and the leaders were within fifty yards of the cannon hidden under that brushwood. Careless heard a muttered order from a chieftain who was with those Indians around the gun. At once that glowing piece of cloth started to move towards the touch-hole.

An arrow stopped him. That Indian slumped by the side of the gun, a feathered arrow sticking out from his side.

It startled those Indians. They looked round

quickly, but they saw no one on the trail except their own Medicine Man.

That chief whirled and saw the cavalry within yards of the gun now, and he knew he had only seconds in which to give that signal to the ambushing Indians.

He jumped and grabbed that piece of glowing cloth and stabbed it towards the touch-hole.

He died, too, before the powder could be ignited.

Another Indian leapt forward – and died.

Two other Indians came wheeling round. They saw their Medicine Man with a bow in his hands and they knew where that death had come from. One leapt for the traitorous Medicine Man while the other tried to explode that gun. The cavalry were within a few feet of the gun muzzle now. Careless, behind his death mask, could see the faces under those broad brims, and he saw that they were suddenly suspicious of what lay hidden in their path.

His arrow transfixed that brown, sinewy hand as it reached towards that touch-hole. Again the smouldering cloth fell to the ground.

Careless heard exclamations from those soldiers across the leafy barrier that covered the gun. They had spotted the gun, and must have seen him standing on that trail. He saw a gun flash up to cover him, and he thought it was a poor way to die at the hands of his own people.

Then that second Indian was at his throat. Careless tried to batter him away, but his movements were restricted by that Medicine Man's clothing. They hadn't been made for a man as big as he.

The two crashed into the dust, that raging Comanche Indian determined to kill the man who had shot down his comrades from behind – even though that killer was his own Medicine Man. Then the death mask rolled off and he saw those features underneath.

His fury seemed to mount to twice its intensity when he saw the paleface in that Medicine Man's garb. His hand came over with a tomahawk. Careless caught it, and flung himself over and sent the naked Indian's body flying on to the trail.

Careless got to his knees just as those cavalry spurred round that gun. He saw the Indian leaping towards him and he threw his fist forward with all the strength of his body. That Indian seemed to run against it with his stomach, and he went down gasping and moaning for breath, and out of the fight from that instant.

Careless wheeled. The cavalry had him covered with their guns. They saw that this was no medicine man, but was one of their own kind. Then they saw him reach for that bow and an arrow lying on the trail. They didn't know what he was going to do, but they saw him string that arrow and then despatch it towards them.

That Indian who had had his arm impaled by an arrow fell back lifeless. Careless had seen him crawling again towards that touch-hole with the smouldering cloth.

Now the last of the Indian gun team was out of action, and that meant that the signal for the slaughter to begin would not sound out. Careless beckoned frantically to the cavalry to come riding on. As the leading officer – a captain of scouts, rode up, Careless called, 'Keep ridin', cap'n! Get them troops out of that valley as quick as' you can!'

In a few shouted words he told them of the danger – of those Indians poised on the heights only waiting for a signal to open fire on the massed ranks below. Their only chance was to bring the troops through the pass at top speed before the ambushers tumbled to the fact that their plans had gone wrong.

He also shouted that ahead of them was a good half of the Comanche force. The captain bellowed orders which were relayed right down that trail. At once the horses leapt to life and came thundering out of that pass.

Up on the heights Indians began to rise from their cover, startled and wondering what to do. But they had been told not to open fire and betray their positions until that cannon roared. They were still waiting for it to go off!

Only when the guns of the artillery were thundering through did they realize that the trap had been neatly sprung, and their victims were getting away. Some arrows began to fire towards those charging gun teams.

All along the heights now was alive with Indians. Safely out of the pass, the colonel, who had come riding up, ordered some of the militia to turn and set up a covering fire to protect their comrades charging through the death pass with the field guns.

There was a crackle of rifle fire which became a sustained fusillade. The Indians on the heights began to scream their war whoops, but the fire was so intense that they had to retreat from the cliff edge. and that gave the artillery a chance to crash through the pass with little harm.

The scout captain had held back the forces about a quarter of a mile along the trail. He was shouting to the colonel that he could see the Comanches sitting their horses in a wood below. The colonel and his officers came racing up to see this new danger. The Comanches were taken completely by surprise. Careless, in his Medicine Man's rig, stood aside and watched the cavalry form up and go charging forward in a devastating ride. He saw the battle begin under those trees, and from the start he knew that the Comanches weren't going to win. That ambush now was against the Indians; for nearly half their force was up on those heights and unable to come down and help the main body.

The artillery got their guns into position and began to fire over the heads of the fighters in that wood. It had no serious effect against the Indians except to alarm them and make them feel that they were up against a too-formidable enemy.

All the same, all that afternoon they fought, fiercely and bravely, retreating all the while, but never giving in.

Then they were driven out on to that great plain and there the superior weapons of the white man decisively turned the battle. Everywhere Indians began to stream away towards the hills where they might expect to find safety.

The cavalry gave them no respite. Careless saw the flash of sunlight on drawn swords and saw charge after charge as the cavalry smashed into fierce-fighting bands of braves. Before darkness the Comanches were completely routed. By night, all had fled and it was safe enough for the troops to light great fires on that plain and rest in security until the following morning.

Careless didn't stay with the troops. When he saw that he could do nothing to help in the battle as he knew that thanks to that ambush being evaded the American troops were bound to win, he got out of his Medicine Man's clothing and began to climb the mountainside.

He realized when he set off that he was unarmed, so his first act was to find those thorn bushes in which he had met the Border adventurers. After searching around for some time he found his rifle and revolvers where they had thrown them.

He was relieved to feel his trusty weapons in his hands again. He didn't want to run into any straggling Comanches unarmed.

He suddenly thought: 'I don't want to run into Major Abigay unarmed, either!'

He wondered what had happened to the major. Wondered where he had got to, and he found himself frowning. Abigay was a very desperate man, and desperate men did things that saner men wouldn't have dreamed of.

As he climbed through the woodlands he thought of Abigay. Abigay couldn't go back to the American army, because he, Careless, had enough evidence against him to get him shot. And he would have to give that evidence, O'Connor knew.

Abigay wouldn't be safe anywhere where white men lived, and in this Comanche country there was no room for a white man in red man's territory. He thought, 'Abigay ain't got no chance at all. He's bound to go under an' I guess he must know it, too. Guess I'd better keep my eyes peeled for Abigay.' And all the way up that mountainside he was watching not so much for bronzed-bodied red men, but for the blue-shirted Abigay. He never saw him.

He climbed out on to the bare hillside above the tree line, and found that dry rain gully and went clambering up it. He was sweating and tired and thought it would be good when he had horseflesh between his knees. Then he came out where the landslide had occurred, where the black, gaping hole marked the cave in which he had left the girl and their horses. As he was walking towards it he thought, 'Why isn't she keepin' watch for me?'

Because it would have been natural with the sound of battle on that far plain below for the girl to be standing at the cave-mouth looking out.

But she wasn't. Even before he entered that cave a foreboding griped him – that he would find it empty when he got inside.

TEN

ALL THINGS END

He wasn't quite right in his surmise. There was one horse standing within that cave – his own. But the girl's horse had gone and she with it.

He took his horse by the bridle and walked it outside. His face looked grim. He knew she wouldn't have left this cave without good cause, and good cause suggested danger to herself.

His eyes swept that wooded terrain beneath him. He looked once at the plain where the fight between the U.S. troops and the Indians was raging. Then his eyes flickered eastwards.

Suddenly he saw Jane Frazer as her horse bolted from the cover of a small copse and he realized that she was riding desperately towards the trail at a point beyond those high cliffs.

He swung into his saddle, still watching. Other figures emerged from that copse, in hard pursuit of the girl. He counted – there were five of them. He didn't need to be told who they were. He started down that mountainside, riding recklessly because of the danger that threatened this fine, attractive girl. As he rode he was trying to work it all out.

The fact that his horse had been left in that cave supplied him with the clue to it all. She must have been standing out there, watching the battle, and those five Border adventurers must have seen her and started up towards her. Jane's only chance would be in flight and she must have taken to her horse immediately and now was trying to out-distance her pursuers.

But as he rode down that steep mountainside towards the tree line, he realized that her enemies weren't being out-distanced. It was only a question of time before she was stopped by the river and then they would catch up with her.

He saw her reach the trail, and after that his view of the chase was intermittent because of the thick border of trees that lined the wagon track.

Just at the moment when he was about to plunge into the woods himself, his eyes lifted and looked towards that charred settlement that marked the ford across the Rattlesnake River.

The sight that greeted his eyes almost brought him to a halt in shock. Strung out across that ford was a long line of mounted Indian warriors.

The girl was riding as hard as she could straight

towards their enemies!

Careless set his heels into his horse's sides and sent it plunging recklessly through the under-growth towards that trail. And yet he knew even as he started that he didn't have a chance of catch-ing up with the girl and warning her of the danger ahead. All he could do was ride and hope for the best.

As he rode he cursed beneath his breath. It was just bad luck for the girl that this band of strag-glers from the battle the day before should be returning now. They were probably quite unaware of the fight which was still going on over the ridge.

Careless swung down on to the trail after a couple of miles' hard riding among the trees. He rode over a hill, and had another glimpse of the scene ahead. He saw Jane breaking from cover and heading across the open ground towards the ford. Then he saw her rein in and knew she had seen those Indians, now climbing out of the river on to the west bank.

Then Jane turned and began to ride back along the trail. Now she was riding towards the enemies she had been fleeing from, but she must have known that she had no chance against the Indians whereas now those five adventurers represented a kinship and possible safety.

Jane worked it out shrewdly. The triumphant yells of those Border adventurers at sight of her hurtling madly back towards them, changed to dismay when they realized why she had turned.

They saw a band of approximately twenty Indians, flat upon their ponies, their war bonnets and lance pennants streaming with the speed of their passage, racing straight towards them.

They forgot about the girl. Her value to them was nothing now. The only thing that counted was saving their skins.

They lifted their guns and began to fire. The girl rode right through those five horsemen and came racing along the trail towards where Careless O'Connor was aproaching on his mighty steed.

Careless could see it all now, Jane fleeing desperately on her tired mount towards him. Those five men frantically trying to turn and come after her to escape from those avenging Indians.

And those Indians, shouting their war-cries and descending upon the Border adventurers at a speed too great to give them any chance to escape.

There was a crash as the Indians rode on to those five desperately fighting men. For a few precious seconds the race was halted while the Indians tore those adventurers from their saddles and slew them. Then a few Indians came round the fighting pack and took up the pursuit of the white girl again.

Careless, riding madly towards the girl, his rifle clutched to his side ready to open fire when he could do so without hitting Jane, suddenly saw Jane leave her saddle and go hurtling into the dust of the trail.

Something had happened to her horse. Perhaps it had stopped an arrow, or perhaps it had just tripped and gone down. But it didn't rise. Jane was out there on the trail in front of those war-whooping Indians, dismounted and helpless.

She began to run towards Careless' thundering horse. It became a race as to who should reach her first – that band of bloodthirsty Indians, or this man intent on saving her life.

They came together at speed. Then Careless opened up with his Sharps and that brought confusion among the pursuers, because no one wanted to be in front and stop a deadly bullet. It threw the Indians back for vital moments. Careless rode up in a flurry of pebbles and a mighty cloud of dust as his horse slithered to a halt. He shouted, 'Jump, Jane!'

Jane leapt for his arms and he put her across his saddle bow, and then he brought his horse's head round and began to race back down the trail.

Those Indians were after him in a moment. Now his rifle was empty and, burdened by the girl before him, he was unable to take accurate aim with his Colt.

The horse was gallant but it was tired and now its stride faltered under the double weight. The Indians were overhauling them.

Careless looked ahead and saw that pass which was to have been a death trap. He thought of the three or four miles that lay between him and the American troops – and safety. And he knew they could never do it. His horse couldn't last more than another half-mile or so at this pace. It was bound to crack up.

But he knew that even before it cracked up these Indians would have overtaken them and they would have gone down before the fury of their onslaught just as those five desperately fighting Border adventurers had gone under.

It wasn't a pleasing prospect. Careless had never been in such a desperate situation. He thought, 'This is one spot I can't figger a way out of!'

Now they were riding between high cliffs, and the echo of their thundering hoofs grew to a tumultuous sound as the Indians streamed into the defile after them.

Now the Indians were so close that their blood curdling war-cries were loud in their ears.

Jane turned and looked up at him. She smiled. It did him good to see her courage at that awful moment.

Then he heard her say, 'This is the end, Careless!'

It was the end and he knew it but he wouldn't admit it. He was a fighting man and he never stopped fighting.

Even now he would ride on until those Indians surrounded him, and then he would fight until there was no more fight left in him.

But he wouldn't give in. That wouldn't be Careless O'Connor.

The girl recognized his thought by the jut of his jaw and by the hard glint to those narrowed grey eyes that searched ahead along the trail – that searched for hope and saw none.

The Indians weren't more than fifty yards behind now. They were thundering towards the end of the pass, towards where that gun still stood behind its camouflage of leafy branches.

Careless thought, 'It's muzzle is still pointing towards us.' And then he remembered that it was charged and loaded and ready primed for firing.

It was right at that moment when that thought came to his mind that he saw a movement alongside the trail. Something blue appeared from the screen of bushes beside that gun.

His heart leapt. Perhaps here was hope – perhaps here were soldiers who might turn the tables on their enemies.

But even as the hope rose in his breast, it was dashed away by sight of that blue-uniformed figure.

A lean man stepped out on the trail – a man

who was dishevelled and hatless.

Major Abigay!

Jane and Careless saw that lean, vengeful figure run towards the cannon. Suddenly Careless saw a thin whisp of blue smoke and at once he shouted. 'Abigay's going to fire that gun!'

They were riding towards the muzzle of that gun. Riding straight on to it and only thirty or forty yards from it now. They couldn't change their tactics, either – they simply had to ride towards that cannon that had brought them so far west. The Indians were within twenty yards of them now and catching up fast. Careless felt his horse stumbling and weakening with every stride beneath him.

They caught a glimpse of Abigay's face over the brushwood that partly concealed the gun. It was ablaze with triumph. Abigay, off his head now because of his brooding, insane passion and heedless of the danger those Indians represented to him, was thirsting for his moment of vengeance. This man O'Connor had brought him to the condition he now found himself in – a man without friends in the world, a renegade who would find no place with his own people, but only disgrace and death.

Abigay the Killer was going to kill the man who had revealed him for the blackguard and villain he was.

The major turned and his hand stabbed out

towards the touch hole. They saw the glowing tinder being applied.

Careless seemed to lift his horse with his legs and throw it to one side of the gun as they raced up. Then the horse stumbled and they all went rolling into the dust.

But at that instant, just when those Indians were lifting their savage voices in triumph at sight of them stumbling and falling, that cannon blazed off.

That cannon which had been the deadliest weapon in all the Mexican dictator's artillery, couldn't miss at that range.

Jane turned her head away quickly, moaning, because now there were no more pursuing Indians. Only a few who pulled their horses round and fled in terror.

The echoes from that gun blast were still reverberating between those cliffs. The sound was stunning to their ears. But even without looking round Careless knew that his enemy, Abigay, had unwittingly disposed of those other savage enemies, the Indians.

He leapt for his horse and caught it because in its terror at the noise it was trying to run away. Jane ran up to him and he threw her into the saddle, and then he looked round.

The smoke was clearing. Riderless ponies were climbing to their feet and going back down that pass now. Other ponies were lying where they had fallen, not moving.

Stunned and wounded Indians, thrown from their terrified mounts, were feebly moving, but the fight seemed to be out of them.

Then Careless saw Abigay. The major was looking over the breech of the gun, and his face was incredulous. He couldn't understand how his enemy had managed to escape death yet again.

Then Abigay came lurching round from behind the cannon. He had a gun in his hand, a heavy Service revolver.

Careless went for his Colt, and then realized that it was useless, that he had emptied it among those Indians, riding along the trail.

They were helpless, faced by a vengeful killer armed with a six-gun.

The major knew it. He wanted to savour this moment of triumph, and instead of shooting immediately he began to walk slowly towards O'Connor. He almost shouted, 'You can't always escape me, O'Connor. I'm goin' to kill you an' this gal, an' then no one knows a thing agen me. I'll still be Major Abigay!'

That was all he wanted – to be Major Abigay. And the way was still clear for him – if only these two witnesses to his infamy were to be removed.

The triumph that filled his soul at sight of his helpless enemies, at the thought of how after all he could save himself by their death, made his hand that held the revolver tremble.

But still he couldn't despatch them. Still there were things he wanted to know.

He exclaimed. 'Before you go out, O'Connor, tell me the secret of this gun! Why have men tried to get it? Why have they killed each other and died for it?'

He was an artillery officer, and yet there were things he didn't know. Careless, his hands held aloft, was watching an Indian who stirred along the trail. That Indian was looking at Abigay, and there was hatred in those brown, pain-filled eyes. This was an Indian who was not going to live, and he couldn't forgive the author of his death – that man in the hated blue uniform of the American forces.

Careless started to speak. It didn't matter if Abigay did know the secret of the cannon.

'That gun was made by an artillery genius for Napoleon. It was an experiment which was tried out in the field, but the Spaniards unfortunately captured it. They didn't know what a prize they'd got. All they knew was they'd got a weapon that shot more accurately than any other they had known.

Looking back along the trail, Careless realized that the Indian was now crawling towards a bow. Jane must have noticed it, too, for he could feel her standing close against his side, and her hand was gripping into his shoulder so that it hurt.

Careless went on with his story. 'When the

Spanish king thought to set up his empire in Mexico, that prize gun was shipped ahead of him. It was added to the Mexican artillery when Santa Anna led a revolt and became dictator. But they knew little about artillery, and they didn't realize what a prize they had. And by now Napoleon had been defeated, and his artillery expert was dead. But the fame of that gun was still known in Europe, and the agent of a mighty power sent emissaries to the American continent to try to get it.'

Into Jane Frazer's mind leapt the name, Reiffel. He would be this representative of a Foreign Power.

That Indian had found his bow, and lying there was pulling a feathered shaft on to the thong.

'But Santa Anna was defeated by American troops and some filibusters brought that gun over the border into Arizona. You came and took it over, major, but even you didn't realize why this was such an exceptional gun.'

The major got impatient. 'Go on,' he urged. 'What is there special about this gun?'

That feathered arrow was lifting to point towards the back of the major.

Careless licked his lips. He said, 'The barrel is grooved slightly requiring special shaped shot. Those grooved spirals twist the shot to send it spinnin' through the air. It's a very simple device, but it sure made that gun the most accurate cannon known, an' for that reason these Foreign Powers would give millions to learn the secret of it.

'But the United States got to know of this and they too wanted to get this gun where their own artillery experts could examine it. I was sent to bring it in. But by the time I got here, it had been captured yet again, this time by Injuns.'

It was at that moment that Careless realized that no matter who the man was or how murderous he might be, he couldn't stand and not warn him when he was about to be shot in the back.

That bow was taut. Careless suddenly rapped, 'Look out, Abigay!'

Abigay saw the way he was looking. He began to turn. And then he laughed contemptuously. He was a man of great conceit, and it was to be the death of him. He called, 'You don't catch me with that old trick, O'Connor!'

He didn't believe there was danger behind him. Careless began to shout again, but this time he was too late.

Abigay crumpled to the ground. The arrow had found its mark. The problem of Major Abigay was suddenly over.

When they looked at that Indian he had fallen into the dust again.

Widow Thomson kept wiping her hands on her apron, and looking as coldly angry as possible.

She was trying to hide the tenderness in her heart, and her disappointment.

She looked across her kitchen and said to big, lounging Careless, 'You ought to be ashamed of yourself. Here's this fine gal breakin' her heart for you an' you're just ridin' away with that silly ol' gun of yours. Why don't you settle down and marry her?'

Jane was there, laughing at the widow woman's outspokenness. Careless just stood with a slight smile on his lips but didn't say anything.

Jane went over and plucked on his sleeve with her slim fingers and then she said frankly, 'It's quite true, Careless. You know that for me there's no man in the world like you. You know it's what I want more than anything – for you to marry me.'

Careless was looking down into her blue eyes. He knew she was intelligent, and he knew she understood. He liked her for it, because she would accept this decision of his and be brave about it – and eventually find happiness somewhere else.

She smiled gallantly up at him. 'It wouldn't work out, would it, Careless? You're a frontiersman, a rolling stone. You just can't settle down, can you?'

Careless sighed and shook his head. It was true. He said, frankly, 'I reckon I'd make a bad husband for any gal, so why go an' spoil things?'

Jane walked to the door outside which his horse stood ready loaded for the trail. She said, 'This is goodbye, pardner. I shall remember you all my life. Goodbye and may you never run into any more danger.'

There was a sniff at that from the widow woman. 'That would break his heart,' she said acidly.

Then Jane was in Careless' arms. She gave him a kiss – just one – and then he turned and swung on to his horse.

As he rode behind the wagon train that was still taking that precious gun eastwards, he thought, 'I meet the purtiest gals, but I sure have to run out on all of 'em!'

He sighed. Then he thought, 'Sure as eggs get broken, I'll be runnin' into more adventures soon, and there'll be another mighty purty gal in that one, too!'

As always, Careless O'Connor was right.

04/08